HEART OF A DRAGON

Fallen Immortals 2

ALISA WOODS

ISBN-13: 9781095743959

Chapter One

I'm not going anywhere, Lucian Smoke.

Arabella spoke those words to him three days ago, and Lucian had never been so angry with a human in all his five hundred years.

He stretched his wings wide and leaped off the Needle, Seattle's iconic spindly tower. As he swooped down to the sparkling lights of the darkness draped city below, his fatigue showed itself in a desire just to fold his wings tight against his body and plummet to the ground, dashing his brains out on the concrete six hundred feet below. No one would see him coming, but his cloaking would disappear as soon as his not-quite-immortal life was snuffed out.

If he would even die.

With his luck, he'd just be knocked unconscious, a golden dragon splayed across Broad Street for the world to see.

He strained to pull out of the dive, leaving a dust-devil of stray papers and decaying leaves in his wake.

Why? Why wouldn't Arabella Sharp act like any normal woman under the circumstances and stomp away from him, his lies, his lair, and his life? He'd pushed her away, laying bare all his deceit, and she'd just stood there, dripping wet at the side of his pool, sexy to the core in her strength and her determination. She'd seen right through his act and refused to leave him to his fate. He'd been unable to meet her righteousness with any kind of answer worthy of it, so he'd stormed off and sent her things to the guest apartment in the keep. But her singular feat—that one act of defiance at his poolside—scorched him like a dragonfire brand across his heart.

It was something Cara would do.

Goddammit.

Lucian rumbled a deep and bone-rattling roar, soaring low and tight across the cityscape. His frustration enlivened the runes under his skin, making them rise and twitch across his scales, itching for magical release. They wanted to vent his rage that this woman—this senselessly brave woman—had arrowed her way straight into his soul. He was such a damn fool to think he could seduce someone like her and not fall down the precipice with it.

He reached out with his fae-given senses across the darkened streets and into the homes of the residents of his city, giving the magic boiling in his blood some release. He searched for the demons haunting the humans he was supposed to protect. One human among them would have to be sacrificed to protect the rest. One woman to bear a dragonling to keep the peace. The treaty was as much a curse as a blessing to humankind. And to him, Lucian Smoke, Dragon Prince of the House of Smoke… it was simple, mindfucking torture.

He blinked, bleary-eyed as he meticulously checked every soul he soared over. He had spent hour upon hour, too many to count, scouring the city, but the surge of demons seemed to have abated. Not a trace of their sulfurous stench had been found in the last three days. But Lucian was far from convinced this uprising of demonkind had been some fluke that could be safely ignored. And besides, the patrols gave him an excuse—*no*, a completely legitimate *reason*—to stay far from the keep—

A whiff of iron-rich scent crossed his snout.

Vampire.

He banked sharply left, following it. *What the actual fuck?* Vampires were forbidden near humans, in an agreement long-standing—for centuries now—between the dragons who watched over the mortal realm and the covens of bloodsuckers who straddled the mortal and immortal. Vampires lived longer than dragons—they were the longest-lived of the supposed mortal-based races—but they were weak. And pathetic. And generally turned Lucian's stomach with their parasitic reliance on the lifeblood of other creatures.

First demons, and now vampires? *What in holy hell was happening?*

Lucian quickly wove through the tight alleyway canyons, focusing in on the blood-tinged scent trail like a laser-guided missile. A fast turn into a dead-end that stank of rotting vegetables brought him swooping in on the vampire and his prey—a woman, pretty and pale and prone in his arms, her high-heeled pump dangling from a foot suspended in the air as the bloodsucker bent her backward, feasting on the jugular at her neck. Her eyes were already glazed, halfway to death as she whimpered through the body-wracking pleasure the vampires evoked in their victims. Their arousal scents—hers *and* his—filled the alleyway. As if there were fucking happening here, not murder.

Lucian vented his roar, but held his dragonfire in check—he would roast the wretched vamp once the human was free. He decloaked just before landing talons-first on the vampire's back, wrenching him away from the woman and slamming him against the red-bricked wall of the alley. Lucian arched back, shifting fast enough to catch the woman in his now-human arms before she cracked her head on the dirty pavement. She was limp with the death-pleasure the vampires gave, blood still surging from the twin holes in her neck.

The bloodsucker scraped himself off the floor of the alley.

"Stay where you are," Lucian said without looking at him. "If you run, I will hunt you."

The supreme absence of sound spoke of how still the vampire had gone, heeding his warning and freezing in place by the wall.

Lucian wasted no time slicing open his own hand and pressing his dragon blood to mix with the woman's at her neck. He summoned his healing runes as well. But she was nearly drained of blood —she would need to actually take some of Lucian's blood inside her, not simply heal the wound, which was sealed almost instantly. Instead, he opened a new wound, this one across her wrist, and clamped the open wound of his hand across it.

She gasped and cried out and struggled a bit in his arms, finally rousing from the powerful lust haze induced by the vampire, but Lucian held her fast and focused on keeping the two wounds free from clotting, so the blood could flow free between them. It was intimate, in a way, this exchange, his blood filling her veins, bringing her back from the brink of death. It would extend her life for years, even with the little he was giving her. She wouldn't need much —his blood would quickly regenerate, replacing the amount she had lost and reviving her soon enough.

"Have any of that to spare?" the vampire asked wryly from his spot by the wall.

"Shut the fuck up," Lucian growled. His words were meant for the bloodsucker, but the woman was recovering fast enough to be frightened by him. As she had every right to be—he was massive next to her slight build, he had an iron grip on her, and there was no doubt he was a predator. Plus she probably mistook the hatred in his eyes as directed at her, the soft beauty in front of him, rather than the beast behind him.

He softened his voice. "It's all right. I'm not going to hurt you." It was a whisper, but he was sure she heard it, given his face was close enough for them to exchange breath. She was soft and smelled of honey and lemons and had a gentle beauty about her. She was the kind of woman he could easily see bedding, and his magical taste of her in this intimate hold—skin-to-skin, blood-to-blood—said she was well-experienced and would ride him until the sun rose. But she was soft in other ways than just appearance—untested by the world, living an untroubled life that meant things had come easy to her. Too easy. She had no battle scars. No darkness. No hard edges that she showed to the world as armor to protect the softness inside.

She would never survive a sealing, much less a dragonling.

She was nothing like Arabella.

The mere fact of that thought tormented him. But the simple truth was that a woman like this held no allure for him—she couldn't fulfill the treaty, and just filling his bed seemed inconsequential next to the sweetness he'd tasted with Arabella. Love blotted out all other things, like the sun driving you blind with its brightness. He knew that all too well. And the price to be paid for it. The things love had driven him to do.

The woman got her feet under her and tried to struggle away. There was enough strength in it that Lucian let her stand on her own. She managed it, twisting an ankle with her high heels, but recovering and stumbling away, throwing fearful wide-eyed glances his way. The vampire was long forgotten in the haze and the shadows.

Lucian watched and waited. When she was gone, he turned back to the bloodsucker.

In a flash instant, he had him pinned to the wall, one hand clamped around the creature's neck, the other pulled back and shifted to claws. "You've picked a bad day to cross me, *vampyre.*"

"Oh? There's a good day to meet a dragon in an alley?" His eyes were all pupil, the inky depths of a vampire well-fed. Vampire eyes were normally black anyway, with the thinnest of red lines showing around the edge, but the pupils expanded when they'd slaked their thirst for blood. Lucian knew the vampire need for blood was a curse, not a choice—they were distant cousins to witches and wolves, with a magical mutation even further back in time that split them off that evolutionary tree of magical creatures. Lucian couldn't rightly blame the creature for *desiring* the woman's blood—that bloodlust was encoded in his DNA—but slaking that lust… that was what animals were for. The drinking of human blood had ceased hundreds of years ago—the condition under which his ruling House had allowed the vampires to live. Many had perished soon after, refusing to drink the blood of animals. Given the sexuality involved in feeding, Lucian supposed he could understand that. The rest had found a way to hunt animals and drain their blood, supposedly in a civilized, less disgusting manner. Then they'd gone into voluntary banishment, deep inside forests where the wildlife still ran free.

As a result, there weren't many covens left… and Lucian didn't recognize this particular vampire at all. He narrowed his eyes, examining the creature more closely. He had a freshness about him, a youth that could be the recent feed or, more disturbingly, that he was newly turned.

"Who's your sire, bloodsucker?" Lucian asked, leaning closer and flexing his talons. Vampires were forbidden from creating more of their species by transferring their cursed blood. Either this one was recently purebred, an uncommon occurrence, or the covens were breaking even more laws than he knew.

The vampire lost his cocky attitude and flattened himself further into the wall. "I am *purebred.* You cannot... you have no cause to..."

"No cause?" Lucian hissed in his face, dragonfire leaking out with the words.

The creature's normal paleness whitened even further. Lucian could justify the vampire's death if anyone cared to hold him accountable. The creature was in breach, not Lucian. But something was very wrong about all of this... and finding out what was going on in his city was more important than shredding a single vampire and reducing him to ash.

Lucian breathed dragonfire in the creature's face, making the bloodsucker squirm. "You would have *killed* that woman had I not intervened."

"No! I promise. I was only... *enthralled.* Just for a moment. I wouldn't have drained her, I swear!"

Lucian huffed. "Just a taste, right?" He should just slay this monster now.

The vampire's face opened with something like hope, and he nodded, rapidly. "She enjoyed it. You saw. And besides... she wanted this. It was a voluntary transaction!"

Lucian was halfway to squeezing down on the vampire's neck when his words registered through his bloodlust. "Voluntary?" What the hell was he talking about?

"Yes, yes!" he gushed. "She was a fetish seeker. Online. Wanted a true vampire experience." The vampire smirked. "It's always the quiet ones, you know?"

Lucian snarled, but he'd tasted that much about the woman for himself. She was an adventurous lover—it was possible she had sought out some kind of sex play. And she would never have suspected she would snare a *real* vampire.

Then the rest of the vampire's words sunk in. *"Always?"* Lucian tightened his grip until the vampire's eyes bulged. One more squeeze... "Is this a sport you engage in often? Luring women to their near, if not absolute, deaths? I'm thinking the world is better off with one less vampire taking advantage of the innocent and unwary. And maybe I need to clear out your coven, as well."

The vampire was protesting, but he couldn't make any sound with Lucian's grip closing down. He watched as blood suffused the dying vampire's face—blood that belonged to that woman, not this foul creature. He almost didn't notice the rustling of wings behind him.

"Let him go, my brother."

Lucian snarled and twisted to face his brother. *Leksander.* "He nearly—"

"I know," he said calmly, with a disgusted look for the struggling vampire in Lucian's grip. "We caught one feeding yesterday."

"What?" That was enough to make him lean back and drop his hold. The bloodsucker fell to the ground, gasping and pawing at his neck.

"It's obviously a problem." Leksander stepped forward and gripped the vampire's arm, hauling him off the ground. The creature's eyes were wide again, struggling against Leksander's hold, even though it was futile. Leksander eyed him coolly. "And a dead vampire can't deliver a message as well as a live one."

Lucian frowned, not sure what his brother intended. Then Leksander placed his hand on the vampire's forehead, and the bloodsucker began to convulse. Lucian took a step back, watching his brother work. The runes were in a frenzy across Leksander's skin, running down his arm to the hand pressed against the vampire's head, then racing back again. Leksander's face was intent on the vampire's, and the creature jerked and twitched as if being electrocuted. It went on and on and on… until finally, Leksander released him, and the vampire fell to the pavement in a heap. He was gasping, and struggling to stay up on all fours, but he was clearly still alive. And when he looked up— the wide, infinitely-dark pupils were gone. *And he had blue eyes.* His scent had changed… he seemed positively…

"Human?" Lucian asked, turning to Leksander. He had no other words.

His brother nodded. "Erelah has been helping me channel my inner fae."

Lucian's eyes were wide, but he held his tongue with the vampire present. Or, he guessed, *human,* now.

"Go," Leksander commanded the man. "Tell your coven that if we catch any more vampires feeding on humans, they won't be cured… they'll be summarily executed. They may feed upon animals if that's their wish. But if there are some among them who wish to put the curse of vampirism behind them, as you have, they may seek an audience with the House of Smoke. Am I clear?"

The man nodded, shakily, and clambered to his

feet. He almost fell twice in his haste to leave, turning the corner of the alley quickly.

Lucian's mouth was still hanging open when he turned back to his brother. "You can cure their curse? When did that happen?"

"While you were busy not sleeping and obsessively searching the city for demons." His brother's cool gaze was now trained on him.

Lucian winced under it. He was the crown prince, and supposedly, the one entrusted with making calm, rational decisions for the realm. He should have thought of sending the vampire back to his coven with a warning. Even without the enticement of a cure, the House of Smoke could certainly enforce the agreement—with dragonfire, if necessary. Instead, Lucian had been willing to squeeze the life out of a being that had no chance against him.

Lucian stared at his boots in the dark Seattle alley. He was too distracted.

"You just need some sleep," Leksander said as if reading his mind, even though not in dragon form. "Where is Arabella?"

Lucian's head snapped up. "At the keep. Unless she's realized her foolishness and decided to leave." But the idea of that stabbed through him.

Leksander's eyes narrowed. "You can't keep her locked in the guest apartment forever."

"She's not locked in!" Lucian growled and dropped his gaze to his quickly-healing hand, absently wiping the smear of blood from it. "I've done everything I can to get her to leave. Cinaed is watching over her, ready to drive her away at a moment's notice. Whenever she comes to her senses."

"Which is why you're flying non-stop patrols."

Lucian lifted his gaze to glare at his brother.

"You can't keep this up," Leksander said, meeting his glare.

"I can keep it up longer than she can."

His brother just shook his head. "I doubt that. Just send her away."

"I tried that." Lucian looked away, down the alley, at the electric glitter of the city at night.

"You're not fooling me, Lucian." His brother's voice was cool and damn aggravating. "Or her, either, it seems. If you truly wanted her gone, she would be."

He slowly turned to face his brother. "Have I told you to fuck off recently? I feel like that's in order again." But his words didn't have much venom in them. The truth was he'd spent himself already in his feeble attempts to push her away. The danger wasn't that he would force her out—the danger was that he would fall into her arms all too easily again. But Lucian wasn't ready to release her into the human world, simply because he wasn't sure it was safe. The fae prince of the Winter Court had already expressed far too much interest in her. If Lucian sent her away, maybe Zephan would lose interest in her... or perhaps he would consider her fair game. And the idea of that... *No.* Nothing could force him to risk her life with a sealing, but he couldn't stand the idea of her trapped in the fae prince's bed, with the endless mindfuckery—and just general fucking—that would happen there. So Lucian was allowing her to stay, doing something he shouldn't... giving her hope.

Leksander held up his hands, a conciliation that also took in the alley walls around them. "Things are going to hell fast in Seattle, Luc. You need to focus."

Lucian grunted. "I can see that with my own eyes. I don't need a lecture from you."

"No. You need a kick in the ass. Leonidas volunteered, but I told him Erelah would want the honors."

A small smile twitched Lucian's lips, just for a

moment. "You know, when it comes to the end of things, maybe I'll call on your angelfire girl and her holy blade. Make quick work of it."

"Lucian, for the love of magic—" But Leksander's expression wasn't worry about Lucian's morbid thoughts; it was disgust. Which Lucian absolutely deserved for forsaking his duty.

He sighed and looked away again. It was incredibly self-indulgent even to consider going wyvern when the fate of the mortal world depended on him getting his shit together and producing a dragonling.

"You need to put an end to it," Leksander said, his voice gruff. "Find another woman to fulfill the treaty. Be done with it."

"I know." But the thought of it filled his throat with bile. "I will. After a few more patrols." Then he shifted and leaped into the air, ignoring his brother's protests below.

Of course, Leksander was right. Lucian needed to bury himself in another woman's scent—seduce her and use her to forget Arabella. And to fulfill the treaty, even if it cost that woman her life. Because the fate of humanity rested on it, and for that, one woman's life—or as many as it took to produce a dragonling—was the price the humans would have to pay. It was Lucian's fate to be the executioner. And once it was done, he would allow the torment of that to drive him wyvern, even with the gift of another five hundred years from his dragonling. The next Dragon Prince would have to endure the curse of his species and the treaty on his own.

Yes, a price had to be paid for peace… but the fates couldn't force him to make *this woman*—Arabella—be the one to pay it.

He'd already sacrificed his heart for the world once; he wasn't going to do it again.

Chapter Two

THE RIDE IN LUCIAN'S BIG BLACK SEDAN WAS smooth as glass.

Arabella was riding shotgun to Cinaed's tensely-hunched form in the driver's seat, but this wasn't the stretch limo they'd taken to Seattle the last time, and Lucian wasn't in the car with them. Nor was he in the keep, as far as she could tell during her wanderings with Cinaed as her shadow. Not that Lucian's right-hand-dragon was any use—the man barely spoke. Not in the keep. Not in Arabella's expansive guest apartment. Not during this long, two-hour drive to Seattle.

The silence was making her skin itch.

"For the love of God, Cinaed," she said, finally,

all in one breath. "Please say *something.* More than two words."

"No, thank you." He kept his eyes glued to the road.

Her groan was inarticulate, near-madness. She reached across the bench seat and pounded her fist into his mountain-sized shoulder. It was like smashing her hand into granite, but she gritted her teeth to not let out the small yelp of pain that caused.

Cinaed winced and cowered into the door, but she couldn't imagine she actually hurt him in any way. His dazzling green eyes roved over her like he thought she was crazy. *And she was.* Three days of stifling silence would drive anyone mad. Three days of trying to hunt down Lucian to get him just to *talk* to her. And nothing to show for it except Cinaed's stoic face staring balefully at her.

She let her hand fall to the seat between them. Maybe she was an idiot to think Lucian Smoke actually loved her and was just pushing her away because he was broken by the loss of his mate. He'd done nothing to confirm her thoughts about that. In fact, he'd done nothing at all except let her stay at the keep when she'd refused to leave.

"I'm sorry," she whispered, still staring at her hand. "I shouldn't have hit you."

A small muffled sound came from the driver's seat. She looked up. Cinaed's eyes were crinkled at the corners, and his mouth was twisting, fighting a smile, even as his gaze was locked on the road.

"You are fucking laughing at me." She contemplated hitting him again.

"Aye." He threw her a smirk.

"Because I have a weak-ass punch, and you're a freakishly strong dragon?" She seriously wanted to smack that smirking face, even if it broke her knuckle.

"Because it took you three days." His smile went broad. "I thought sure you'd be slitting my throat in the middle of the night by the second one."

So he *knew* how frustrated she was. *Of course, he did.* The whole keep had to be laughing at her ridiculous stubbornness in sticking around for a dragon—their *prince,* no less—who obviously didn't want her. He had flat-out rejected her, and she was just hanging around like a love-sick puppy.

Her mind flashed back to the girl who had been in Leonidas's apartment. These guys were so gorgeous, they had to have stalker-women after them all the time. Arabella was probably just the latest nutjob who wouldn't leave.

Her shoulders dropped as the rest of the fight went out of her. She folded her arms across her chest and stared out the windshield. The morning sun was bright, no clouds for a change, and it seemed like everything in Seattle glittered with newness. She squinted against it, irrationally angry at the city for gleaming while her thoughts were so mired in darkness.

The silence stretched inside the car as the tires chewed through the miles and brought them nearer the city. What the hell was she thinking? It seemed all romantic and grand-gesture-ish when she proclaimed her determination to stay, but since then, she'd been mired in second- and third-guessing. Did she really love Lucian Smoke? She'd known the man for less than a couple weeks. Was she really ready to sign up for mating for life?

She had vowed not to leave the keep until he stopped ignoring her, but Lucian wasn't even at the keep right now—he would probably never know she had left. This was just a short run to the city, then she'd be back at the keep, but her law practice definitely needed her. The scanner had broken down, and their shoestring budget didn't have tech support. Just her friend Rachel, and she was frankly terrible at it. That was actually Arabella's job. In fact, *all* of it was her job, and she was falling woefully behind. She and Rachel had been juggling things over the phone and the computer, but Arabella needed to tell her best friend that she'd be staying indefinitely at the keep.

Unless that was utter foolishness.

Maybe she should just cut her losses and have Cinaed drop her at her small hole of an apartment where she would get on with the business of forgetting the hot dragon shifter who had swooped into her life and changed what she knew about the world —and men—forever. It was obvious that Lucian's love for her—if it was ever really that strong in the first place—wasn't strong enough to break through the darkness that was plaguing him.

She sighed and blinked into the sunshine. She was a fool to think *she* was the woman who could cure him of the pain from his past. That much was obvious. She should probably clear out and make way for a woman who might be able to do that for him.

"Don't give up, my lady." Cinaed's voice was soft, the teasing completely gone.

She jolted a little, not expecting him to speak.

"What? I thought you were…" She gestured vaguely at his bulky form in the driver's seat, dressed in the same formal clothes as he wore to the city before—a beautifully cut suit, white starched shirt, and black tie. "I thought you couldn't wait to get me out of the keep. To send me home so you could stop babysitting me." From the beginning, Cinaed had made it clear that he would drive her home at any moment, she just had to say the word. Those were Lucian's orders, and Cinaed had never given a hint that he disagreed with them in any way.

"I've been forbidden to talk to you about my prince. Or the treaty. Or… anything really." Cinaed held her gaze for a long moment before looking back to the road. "I've not been forbidden from encouraging you to stay."

She stared at his profile. His eyes solemnly examined the road. "You think I'm doing the right thing by staying."

"I think I can't discuss the reasons why I think you should stay." He peered at her again. "But you should. Stay, I mean."

She smiled. "So… encouraging me is a loophole in your orders."

Cinaed sighed and looked back to the road.

"Not that it would matter, should the prince find out. Lucian would still have my head on a pike."

"No, he wouldn't," Arabella said, her smile growing. "That's not the kind of dragon he is."

Cinaed raised an eyebrow but said nothing.

Arabella twisted to face him better, propping her arm on the seat back. "So, you can't tell me anything, but I can tell *you* things. And you can let me know if I'm correct."

He frowned. "I don't know about that."

"I know Lucian lost his mate." A giddy rush was filling her. Maybe she could finally get some answers, even if in a round-about way, that could help her decipher the mystery of the Dragon Prince of the House of Smoke. "It was horrible, and he blames himself. He doesn't want to go through that again, and who could blame him? Am I right so far?"

"I can't say anything about that." Cinaed's frown was growing darker.

"I already know all that, Cinaed. The fae prince, Zephan, showed it to me."

He flashed her a wary look but said nothing.

"And I'm not a fool," she added. "Anyone could see how broken he is about her." She swallowed, and all the doubts came flooding back. Who was she to think she could fix something that horrible? Especially when she was so in the dark about everything in this magical realm. "The thing is that all the rest is murky. He said he'd die if he doesn't mate and produce a dragonling... but then he kind of implied that was a lie. I don't know what parts are lies and what is the truth. And he won't talk to me, Cinaed."

The man just gripped the steering wheel tighter and stared straight ahead.

"There's this treaty thing that says he has to produce a dragonling, and somehow the fae are involved in that, and he said something about keeping the realms apart, but I don't really understand any of it. What is this treaty? Can I get a copy of it? I know how to read a contract, Cinaed. Maybe there's a loophole in *that*. Or something..." She stopped because he was wincing and pressing his lips together.

She wasn't getting anything out of him this way.

She softened her voice. "He's hurting, Cinaed. I know that for sure."

He peered at her again.

"He's hurting, and that tears me apart." She swallowed down the tears that were suddenly threatening at the back of her throat. "He told me about losing his mate, and all I could think about was holding him. Stopping the pain in his eyes. Is that love? I'm not even sure I know. Maybe I'm just a sucker for good-looking men in pain." Despair was creeping back into her voice. She could feel it edging darkness into her mind.

Cinaed pulled the car to a stop.

Arabella was startled to see they had arrived at her law office. She blinked back the tears that were hanging out at the corners of her eyes and put her hand on the door to open it. Cinaed stopped her with a touch on her shoulder that quickly vanished. She turned back to him.

His green eyes were intent on her. "I can't tell you anything about my liege, but I can say, without a doubt, that you are a strong woman, Arabella Sharp. A noble one. The kind whose heart beats for others, and who can see things with not just her eyes, but her soul." One corner of his mouth tipped up. "And you're stubborn. The fact that you've stayed at the keep…" His eyes widened like he thought he had said too much, and he dropped his gaze to the seat.

Arabella held her breath, waiting.

He looked up again, his gaze intense. "It says things about you. Things no dragon would miss."

Her heart lurched. *Lucian noticed.* She was just sure that was what Cinaed meant. Lucian might be trying to ignore her, but the fact that she hadn't given up yet was having an impact on him. And if it was having an impact, then maybe she could eventually reach him. Then she could break through his stubbornness and find a way around the walls he'd built to encase his heart like a tomb.

"Then let's make this trip to my office quick," she said with a small smile. "And get back to the keep."

Cinaed's smile blazed forth. He really was a heart-stoppingly beautiful man, with those green eyes and reddish-brown hair and fresh-faced smile. If Arabella's heart hadn't already been taken by the brooding prince, she could fall for the kind heart Cinaed seemed to have as well.

He hopped out of the car and hurried around to her side to open the door.

She was all smiles, a new lift in her heart until she turned to face the front door of her office. *It was open.* And not just open… *broken.* The shiny new hinges had held, but the wood near the top of the doorframe had splintered when the metal hinges had pulled free from the wall, leaving the door at a cant.

"Rachel," she gasped, her feet momentarily frozen to the sidewalk.

Cinaed roared and moved all at once, a blur of black suit as he raced to the door, shoved it open, and tore inside. Arabella unlocked her knees and ran after him. It took a split second for her eyes to adjust to the relative darkness of the office, and in that blind moment, she heard Rachel scream.

"Rachel!" Arabella groped forward, her vision slowly fading back.

A man in a rumpled t-shirt had Rachel up against the wall, the bulk of his body covering her as he held her by the throat. He'd twisted around to see who had slammed through the door.

"Stay back—" the man started to say, shaking a fist at her and Cinaed, but Cinaed had already reached him. With a roar, Cinaed grabbed the man by the neck and yanked him off his feet. Then he slammed the man against the wall and pinned him with his feet dangling. The man clawed at his throat, where Cinaed was quickly choking him to death. Cinaed spared only a single growl for the man before turning to Rachel, still standing stunned next to them, braced against the wall where the man had held her prisoner.

"Are you all right?" Cinaed's voice was gentle for her.

Rachel nodded erratically, eyes wide.

Arabella rushed to her side, gathering her and pulling her away from the wall and the two men. Only then did she recognize the man—he was one of Rachel's many low-life exes, the latest one who hadn't liked her love-em-and-leave-em attitude one bit. His name was Simon, and he'd been stalking her cell phone for weeks, leaving crazy-ass messages. In all of Arabella's personal drama, she'd forgotten. Guilt speared through her as she hugged her best friend.

Rachel was shaking. "I locked the door. I swear I locked the door."

Arabella hugged her harder. "It's okay. You're going to be okay." She answered Cinaed's concerned look with a nod. Rachel was tougher than anyone Arabella knew—she'd recover. It was a sad truth about both their lives that this was far from the first time men had threatened them. Or tried to kill them. Once Rachel had a minute to calm down, and she'd give some serious shit to this asshole.

Cinaed turned back to the man, leaning close and getting in his face. "You disgust me." The snarl was rich with danger. The man's eyes bulged. Cinaed's body blocked most of their view, but Arabella could see his hand—the one wrapped around Simon's throat—had shifted partially into talons.

Oh shit… "Cinaed, don't kill him!"

"The world won't miss the likes of this one." Cinaed's voice was cold.

Simon was clawing desperately at his throat.

Rachel broke away from Arabella's hold around her shoulders and stalked over to the two men. Cinaed glanced at her and lifted an eyebrow—he didn't stop choking the man, but Arabella could see he had shifted his talons back to human fingers before Rachel could see.

She jabbed a finger in the dying man's face. "You fucking asshole! I told you to stay away from me. Maybe now you'll listen!" Her finger was shaking—she curled it into a fist like she might punch Simon in the face, but then she took a step back, every inch of her quivering. Only it seemed more from anger now than fear.

Cinaed was watching her, eyes alight.

She finally met his gaze. "Don't kill him."

"It would give me great pleasure to do so," Cinaed said casually. And the way he was peering into Rachel's eyes, it seemed like there was *more* that would give him pleasure than just slaying the guy who had threatened her. Namely, getting it on with her best friend.

Not again. What was it with these two?

Rachel seemed to be fighting a smile. "I can think of something much more pleasurable—"

"For God's sake." Arabella strode over to interrupt the ogle-fest going on between the two of them. "Let him go, Cinaed," she ordered.

He flicked a look at her, then at Simon. The man's eyes were rolling back in his head.

Cinaed released him, and Simon slumped to the floor, leaning against the wall and gasping. Cinaed curled a lip in disgust. "You're lucky you have your life. Take it and leave. Next time, I'll be quicker and give the lady no choice but to mourn your carcass."

Rachel's eyes were wide, giving Arabella a look that said, *Is this guy for real?*

Arabella knew the feeling.

Simon scrambled to his feet and stumbled out the door, which was still hanging off its hinges.

Cinaed gave his retreating back one last snarl, then turned back to Rachel. Her gaze whipped to him, eyes glittering. "Damn," was all she said, and Arabella knew that feeling, too. But a quickie with a dragon—especially given Rachel didn't *know* Cinaed was a dragon—was not a good idea. Not that there was any danger of Rachel falling in love, the way Arabella had; Rachel left men before the afterglow had even worn off. All by design. She kicked them to the curb before they could do it to her… which was why she had stalkers in the first place. That and some men were assholes. Rachel wasn't any good at picking the good ones, so she had given up trying a long time ago.

Cinaed frowned and lifted Rachel's chin with one finger to peer at her throat. Even Arabella could see the angry red choke marks that were already on their way to becoming bruises. "That demon spawn hurt you," he growled, soft, angry, and low. "You should have let me end his miserable life."

Rachel was practically melting under his touch. She lifted her chin even further, offering her neck to him. "Maybe you should kiss it and make it better."

Cinaed smirked and leaned forward.

Oh, for fuck's sake. "Rachel!"

"Busy here, Ari," she said, not flinching.

But Cinaed froze and flicked a look at Arabella. She nailed him with a glare. She'd already told him once to keep away from Rachel.

He dropped his hand from Rachel's chin and stepped back.

"If Cinaed had killed your asshole boyfriend—" Arabella started.

"This trash was your boyfriend?" Cinaed asked Rachel, the glower coming back to his face.

"*Ex*-boyfriend," Rachel said hastily. "Very much *ex.*" She threw a glare in Arabella's direction.

"Your *ex*-boyfriend is an ass," Arabella replied. Then, to Cinaed, "But if you killed him, how would we explain that to the police?"

Cinaed sighed but didn't argue.

"And when you said *demon spawn…*" Arabella gave him a pointed look. Did he mean literally demon? Because if Rachel's ex-boyfriends were becoming possessed or whatever Lucian had been talking about with demons in the city…

"A figure of speech," he said, with a glance for Rachel's sharp-eyed stare. "Regardless, I do not trust him not to return." Cinaed scowled at the broken door. "Nor do I approve of the general security of your office."

Well, it was hard to argue with that. In fact… "Rachel." She took her friend by the shoulders and turned her away from drooling over Cinaed. "I don't want you coming into the office anymore.

Not until…" She glanced at Cinaed. He shook his head. "Not until we have some better security measures."

"Yeah, well, that's going to make meeting with clients a tad more difficult."

Arabella flicked a glance to Cinaed again, but she didn't need his confirmation. She knew the House of Smoke had whatever tech wizardry she would need to set up a remote office. And she needed to know Rachel was safe while she figured out this whole thing with Lucian. In fact, having her best friend at the keep might prevent Arabella from going crazy in the meantime.

"I want you to come to the safehouse with me," Arabella said to her.

"What? Why?" Her brow scrunched up.

"There are a few things I haven't told you, Rach," she started.

"I guessed that much." She threw a slanty-eyed look at Cinaed.

"I've got a bit of a situation, and I need your help." Arabella pleaded with her eyes. "It'll only be for a short while, and we can work on the practice together up there. You'll have everything you need, and I won't have to worry about you being safe while you're here, and I'm not."

Rachel frowned at the sudden seriousness of her tone.

"I agree," Cinaed said with a short nod. "It's safer to have you both at the keep."

"The keep?" Rachel asked.

"He means the safehouse." Arabella frowned. "We can tell you about it on the way."

"Wait, McHottie is part of this deal?" Rachel asked with a growing grin. "Why didn't you just say so? Let's go!" She marched toward the door.

Oh man. Arabella was already regretting this. How was she going to keep the two of them out of each other's pants?

Cinaed dropped his voice and leaned close. "What will you tell her about… well, the nature of those at the keep?"

"She already thinks you guys are shifters," Arabella said, matching his whisper voice. "Trust me, she won't care what kind. And besides, that was just one of Lucian's lies, right? The whole swearing me to secrecy thing?"

"It is *not* a well-known fact," Cinaed said, pointedly. "Do you wish your friend to have to endure a forgetting spell?"

Arabella frowned. "You said this was a good idea."

"I said she would be safer at the keep," he said, exasperated. "The rest she needn't know."

"Hey, nice ride!" Rachel said from the door, eyeing Lucian's luxury car outside. "Are you two coming, or what?"

Arabella jabbed a finger in Cinaed's face and whispered, "Remember what I said—no bedding my best friend then telling her that she's not mate material!"

He winced then looked to Rachel. "Wouldn't think of it, my lady." But she could tell by the look on his face that he was *very much* thinking about it.

Arabella would just have to keep an eye on the two of them. She would have her hands full figuring out how to repair Lucian's broken heart—she didn't need to deal with Rachel getting her heart broken as well.

She strode toward her friend waiting by the door.

Chapter Three

L<small>UCIAN WAS SO TIRED, HIS WINGS COULD BARELY</small> carry him back to the keep.

Once he was inside the perimeter spells, the lights of home beckoned. He magically flicked open the rooftop entrance and dropped heavily into the main meeting room, landing as lightly as a sack of rocks. He had shifted on the way down, and his black boots shook the floor enough to rattle the table. The movement made the table's dragon emblem shimmer with the reflected lights softly glowing on the walls. His landing had the grace of a lumbering ox—he was bone weary and ready to collapse in his lair. He'd been gone for days, and it showed most in his human form—three days worth of scraggly beard roughened his face. He needed a shave and a shower and a bed in which to fall—alone. And not in that order. He'd probably slit his own damn throat if he wielded a blade at the moment, even for shaving.

He only managed to drag himself halfway across the meeting room when Leonidas strolled through one of the side doors, picking up his pace when he saw Lucian.

"My brother, whatever it is, surely it can wait—" Lucian tried.

"I thought you might want to know your girlfriend is back." His brother delivered the words with a cool arch of his eyebrow, but they slammed into Lucian like bullets.

"Back?" Lucian hadn't used his fae senses to scan the keep—he'd just assumed Arabella was still in the guest apartment where he'd left her, days ago. "Back from *where?*" His heart was suddenly stuttering in his chest. He braced his hand against the wall, the fatigue making him unsteady.

Leonidas nodded in a knowing way like this was the reaction he expected. "Apparently, she had a little trouble at her office."

Her office? Images flashed through his mind of

that first night when he'd rescued Arabella from that half-demon in an alley near her office. "What the hell is Cinaed doing, taking her back there?" Lucian's words were a slurred growl.

"Exactly what you asked him to do?" Leonidas's eyes narrowed. "He took her away when she wanted to leave. Unfortunately, he also brought her back. And now—because of the attack—we have two of them."

"*Attack?*" His vision was blurring.

"She's *fine.*" Leonidas scowled. "Lucian, you should just send her away for good—"

But Lucian was already half-running his way out of the meeting room, leaving his brother's rambling words behind. He rubbed the blurriness from his eyes, but he knew the keep well enough to find Arabella's apartment blindfolded.

He wove his way through the corridors, slowly realizing that he hadn't actually been to the guest apartment in ages—not since Cinaed joined them, bedraggled, barely escaping the House of Fyre. The young blue dragon was his best friend now, but back then he had been sequestered inside the guest apartment until the House of Smoke could decide whether to accept him. He'd fought a noble fight to escape the horrors of his own House, and he was a good and strong dragon—pure of heart in all things. He had won Lucian's friendship early on, but now… now, Lucian's fatigue and the irrational side of his brain teamed together to rage over the fact that Cinaed had actually *let Arabella leave*. Regardless of Lucian's words, he couldn't be sure it was safe yet. Cinaed should've known that.

When Lucian arrived at the door of the guest apartment and waved it open, Cinaed's scent was all over it. A male dragon, marking his territory. With the woman who was supposed to be Lucian's mate.

Lucian stormed in and found Cinaed standing next to the windows with Arabella and another woman. Lucian ignored the teasing scent of Arabella's freshly-scrubbed skin floating across his snout and went straight for his best friend, grabbing him and slamming him against the glass, shaking it and rattling the panes two stories high. Fire leaked out with Lucian's heaving breath, and suddenly he felt something foreign and wild crawling under his skin. *The wyvern.* Not just his normal dragon—the wyvern was a wild beast, the form his dragon would take once his time as a man had expired. The twitching feeling washed over him like panic. The rush of blood-pumping anger had summoned his wyvern.

Holy mother of magic. Lucian desperately tried to hang on to his humanity, but his grip was slipping. His hand—the one shoving Cinaed up against the glass—shifted to razor-sharp talons, biting through his friend's black jacket and into his skin. A wyvern's tail sprouted from the small of Lucian's back and swished behind him.

A red haze clouded his mind. He had to grunt out his words. "Why… did you take her… to that place…"

Cinaed's eyes were wide—concern and horror holding them open. "She was never in any danger, Lucian. *I swear.*" But his gaze flicked past Lucian's shoulders.

Lucian felt his wings spring loose. He was half *wyvern* now, breathing dragonfire on his best friend's face. Losing his grip on rationality. Angry beyond measure. Fighting a beast form he had no way to control.

He swallowed and fought against the wyvern anyway, holding fast to what he was. *I am a prince of the House of Smoke.* He repeated the words like a mantra in his mind, a magical shield against the beast. *His beast.*

Cinaed's sharp-eyed stare grew more concerned. *"My liege,"* he whispered, bringing his hands up to grasp hold of Lucian's shoulders, hard. "Not yet. It's not your time yet."

Lucian gritted his teeth and squeezed his eyes shut, holding back the wild roar building inside him, but it wasn't until he heard a soft whisper of feet on the luxurious white carpet and felt Arabella's gentle hand landing on his scaly arm, that he had any chance at all. Dragonfire still curled from his mouth, but her nearness and her touch and her scent… they calmed him in a way that three days of scouring the streets for demons hadn't. This effect she had on him… he knew the danger of it. But he also knew it was the thin thread pulling him back to his humanity.

His wyvern retreated.

Her hand slipped away, and she took a step back.

He refused to turn to her, keeping his eyes shut and focusing instead on making sure his wyvern was actually contained. The danger of that was incalculable. Once he lost control, there was no guarantee of coming back. Ever since his five-hundredth birthday came and went, he knew he was living on borrowed time. He may not know the day or the hour, but like a human passing their hundredth year, it was a clear, unavoidable fact that a limited number of days remained. Lucian had contemplated slipping into the wyvern state *intentionally*... but this was the first time it had taken hold of him by its own accord. The threat of death had never breathed so fiercely down his neck. Turning wyvern wasn't explicitly death, but losing one's mind to the animal, to the beast... it was death for the human side of him.

He felt the last of the dragon parts of him shift back into human form. When he opened his eyes, Cinaed's face held relief. Lucian released him, then stepped back and shook his head. He was tired. So tired. How long had it been since he'd slept? He'd let it go on too long.

He was a fool.

He grimaced before turning to face the women. Both were wide-eyed. The one standing behind Arabella must be her friend, Rachel— Lucian tasted her anger and rough edges. She was especially horrified at what she'd seen. And rightly so.

Arabella eased toward him again. He shrunk back. Her touch had the power to bring him back from his wyvern form—he had no chance of resisting it in his human one. He was already enveloped in her scent, feeling it pull him in. Her friend Rachel rushed forward and grabbed hold of Arabella's arm, tugging her back.

"What are you doing?" she hissed, eyeing Lucian like the wild beast he truly was. At least, for a moment.

Arabella's beautiful green eyes never left him. "It's all right, Rach. He's not going to hurt me." She shrugged off Rachel's hold and took another step toward him, but then dropped her hand, not reaching for him any longer, just standing tall in front of him. "Are you?"

He didn't bother answering. The man inside him had already vowed to give up everything before allowing anything to hurt her. But the wyvern… that wasn't even *him*. He couldn't make any guarantees.

Cinaed shuffled away from the window and toward Rachel. He slipped a hand onto the woman's shoulder and bent his head close to her ear, whispering something. Rachel's eyes grew a little wider.

Arabella's gaze had followed them.

Cinaed must have talked Rachel into leaving them alone because the two of them quickly scurried out of the great room and toward the back, where the kitchen and eventually the bedroom lay.

Arabella watched them go.

He looked her over while he had freedom from her scrutiny. His eyes drank in every sweet curve of her face, every curl of her lashes, every soft fall of her reddish-tinted brown hair. She was so beautiful. And her scent was intoxicating him.

It was such a mistake for him to come here.

"You left," he said, the strain in his voice still showing the struggle to keep control. He was shocked at how wild and hoarse it sounded. He had to look even worse.

She slowly turned to meet his gaze. "I thought that's what you wanted."

It was like a physical dagger had been stabbed in his chest. His dragon—the human-type beast, not the wild one, not his *wyvern*—writhed under his skin, wanting out. Wanting to drag her back to his lair.

"Yes, I want you to leave!" The screech in his voice alarmed him, but her gaze stayed steady. Unnervingly so. Like she had a will of iron, stronger than magic, stronger than the forces that were tearing him up inside. His mind was scream- ing, *it's safer here, don't let her leave!* The truth, of course, was that he never truly wanted her to leave. In fact, he wanted her back in his lair—that was where his treasure should be. But those voices had to stay inside his head. He fought to make the words that came out of his mouth more sane. "But if you do leave, you shouldn't take unnecessary risks. What is this I hear about a man attacking you? What happened?" His gaze roved over her body, this time not reveling in her soft beauty but searching for any harm done to her. He couldn't see any obvious wounds, and he didn't scent any blood.

But that didn't mean anything. Some wounds weren't visible. He knew that all too well.

"It was one of Rachel's exes—he's an asshole, and he nearly killed her. Cinaed saved her." She had a pinched look now, concerned for her friend, but obviously not for herself.

How so like her. Lucian felt the dragonfire brand across his heart—the one that belonged to her— throb with the sensation of burning again. *This woman…* she was irresistible to him.

He cleared his throat. "So, the asshole wasn't after *you.* This time."

She frowned. "No."

An awkward silence reigned as they stared at each other. He struggled to form the words that needed to be said. "Why did you come back?" The pain was stabbing through him again.

"Because you needed me." She said this with a force of conviction that ripped right through him.

"I do *not* need you." But even he could hear the weakness in it. "You should leave." His breath was becoming labored with the effort of saying these words again. *"Please leave."* Softer, this time. He could see the hurt in her eyes, and if the wyvern didn't kill him, that look just might. "Just… when you do leave, make sure you're safe. Listen to Cinaed. Do what he says. Don't take unnecessary risks."

She took a step toward him and then another. Suddenly, his back was up against the glass.

"You care about me, Lucian, I know you do." She reached out to touch him. He cowered away from her, but she still managed to land one of those soft hands on his body, his bare skin….

He took a deliberate step back, breaking free. He was too tired. Too vulnerable for this. *His wyvern…* he couldn't risk that with her. He had to put some distance between the softness of her skin and his aching need to touch her. It was bad enough when he was in his lair, and she was here— he could scent her across the stretch of the keep— but it was a hundred times worse in her presence.

And he was too tired to resist.

He cleared his throat. "Apologize to your friend for me—for losing control. It won't happen again."

She opened her mouth to say something more, but he turned his back quickly and strode across the great room toward the front door of her apartment.

He needed to find another woman. *And soon.*

Chapter Four

"When you said *dragons*, girl, I didn't think you meant… I mean, *fuck*, Lucian is a crazy, *badass* dragon!" Rachel was eyeing Cinaed like he'd turned into that wild beast that Lucian had been only a few minutes ago. But that wasn't Lucian's true dragon at all! And Arabella's heart was still sliced to pieces from his latest rejection—he had literally told her to leave. *Again.* He practically begged her to do it.

Rachel's stink-eye pointed in Cinaed's direction was getting him red in the face.

"Yes, we're *dragons,*" he said through his teeth. "There's far worse we could be. You have no idea the *things* that are out there. Things my prince is protecting you from." Then he pressed his lips into a flat line, stepped back, and ran a hand through his hair. He threw a quick angry look out the window at the early afternoon sun lighting up mountains around them. He was obviously holding back from saying anything more in front of Rachel. But Arabella needed *more* information, not *less*—and she was certain that Cinaed knew more than he was telling them both.

"You *have* to tell me about the treaty, Cinaed," she said. "That's driving all of this, isn't it?"

"I'm forbidden." He glared at her.

"What a load of crap that is," Rachel threw at him, along with her pointed finger. Then she turned to Arabella. "I don't care if they're dragons or wolves or whatever… they're still *men*, Arabella. They still lie about every damn thing, if it suits them. Or they don't say anything at all when they could easily just explain themselves." She lifted her chin in Cinaed's direction, gauntlet thrown.

He took two fast steps closer to her. "I am an *honorable* dragon, and when I make a promise—" He cut himself off again, his mouth working, like he was chewing on the things he wanted to say but couldn't.

Rachel wasn't backing down a single inch from the tall, muscular shifter as he loomed over her. Arabella didn't know what Cinaed was thinking.

That he might be able to intimidate her? Rachel didn't take shit from anyone. Especially hot men. There was a long line of those in her wake, and it was an endless source of trouble.

Cinaed swung his anger in Arabella's direction. "If you think my prince is not doing the right thing, if you think he's a *dishonorable* dragon, then perhaps you should leave after all."

"No," she replied, the anger dissipating from her voice as she realized what she had to do. "The only place I'm going is where I can get some answers." She chewed her lip and stared out the window for a moment. If Lucian wouldn't talk to her, and Cinaed had been forbidden—

"What do you mean by that?" The anger in Cinaed's face had morphed into a slight panic. "This isn't the time to go after the prince, my lady—"

She held up her hand to stop him. "I know." It carved into her that Lucian was still trying to get her to leave. Maybe she was wrong about every-thing, but she was too stubborn to simply walk away now. Not until she truly understood what was going on. And this treaty was at the heart of it. Whatever had just gone down with Lucian and that crazy dragon form was part of it. That thing was completely unlike his beautiful golden dragon—rough, bony ridges instead of smooth-as-silk scales. It was still golden, but wild and fierce-looking. She didn't know what that was about, but Lucian was obviously struggling with it. He needed time to get himself together.

And she needed time to figure this out, as well.

"You stay here and guard Rachel," she said to Cinaed.

"*What?*" he replied as if she had suggested he jump off a cliff. "I don't follow your orders. And the prince explicitly said—"

"I'll stay in the keep, Cinaed," she said cutting him off again. "But I don't need you following me around like a puppy. Not for what I have to do."

Rachel was frowning at her, but when Arabella gave her a small nod, she picked up that ball and ran with it.

Turning to Cinaed, Rachel took three quick steps to close the distance between them, swaying her hips as she did so. Then she went right for it, sliding her hands up Cinaed's chest and grabbing his head to pull him down for a very hot kiss.

Cinaed's eyes went wide. He tried to pull back, but Rachel had a good hold on him, so he just ended up pulling her with him. Plus her touch had to be sparking some of that red-hot sexual tension the two of them had going ever since they first laid eyes on each other. Arabella smirked and turned to make a run for the door.

Cinaed managed to get his lips free of Rachel well enough to call out to her, "What is your intention, my lady?" But then Rachel's fingers were in his hair, her lips urgently seeking his again, and Arabella had reached the front door.

She slipped out, closing the door behind her, and waiting a moment to see if Cinaed would follow. He must trust her well enough to let her go, probably figuring she was safe in the keep. She didn't hear any pounding dragon boot steps stomping toward the door.

She scurried away down the hall, pulling out her phone to find the GPS location of Leonidas's apartment. She had been there once before, and it wasn't hard to find again. She only hoped that this time, there wouldn't be some hot blonde waiting just inside. Or that Leonidas wouldn't be in the middle of a tumble in the sheets with some other human woman.

When Arabella reached his door, she pounded on it. She waited… and waited… and was ready to pound again, because dammit, it was the middle of the afternoon, and this was more important than Leonidas's sex life. She raised her fist to beat on the door again just as it opened.

A slow grin spread across Leonidas's face as he braced against the door frame and leaned into it, looking her up and down.

"I wondered how long it would take for you to find your way back to my lair."

What did he mean by that? "I have questions," she said with her best no-nonsense lawyer voice. "And this time, I'm not leaving until I get answers." She crossed her arms and planted her feet, just so he would know she meant business.

His eyes sparkled, but he stepped back and gestured for her to come inside.

She unlocked her arms and strode through the door. He closed it behind her, but when she turned back to face him, he was suddenly on her—his lips on hers, his strong muscular body pressed hard against her. One of his hands went around the small of her back with the other in her hair. His tongue was invading her mouth, as he lifted her effortlessly from the floor. He walked her two steps back and pressed her body into the wall. His touch was fiercely strong and demanding and ardent… yet strangely gentle and enticing. He wasn't hurting her, but he was kissing the hell out of her. Her whole body was in shock. And for a half second, her body molded into his, accepting this hot and delicious kiss he was serving up.

Then she came to her senses and pushed him away.

"What the hell, Leonidas?" she demanded breathlessly. Pushing away a dragon was almost impossible—and Leonidas certainly didn't go far. He still had her trapped against the wall, one hand in her hair, the other on the wall next to her head. A slow, sexy smile took over his face again. With the dilation of his pupils, the slightly panting of his breath, his lips still parted, lingering near hers… it was as if he was just taking a breather before starting up again. The scent of him—masculine and earthy and tinged with a little bit of campfire smoke that was both warm and welcoming and dangerously hot—all of it sent an embarrassing flush of heat through her body. It pooled between her legs. How could she be reacting to him like this?

"You've been in my brother's bed," he said, soft and seductive and leaning even closer to brush his lips against her cheek. "You know what it's like to have a dragon for a lover. I promise you, my bed would be every hot, wet dream you've ever had.

You don't need Lucian. Trust me when I tell you I've had far more experience, and I can be that lover who would satisfy your every wish."

Her hands were still planted against his chest, pushing him away, but they weakened a little. His words were heating her body in a way that was confusing her brain. That scent of his kept washing over her.

He leaned closer and whispered even more seductively in her ear, "Whatever it is you want, Arabella, I can give it to you. There's no physical thing you'll ever be denied. I will worship every inch of your body. And if it's love you want, my sweet, sweet Arabella, you will have my complete and utter devotion all the days of your life."

What was this madness—this lust haze—that was clouding her brain? She renewed her efforts to push him away. He was like a granite mountain in front of her, but he did ease back enough to look her in the eyes.

She finally got her mouth working again. "How can you do this?" She put as much disgust into that question as she could.

Only now he was capturing her with those blazing blue eyes, drilling into her with a look every bit as seductive as his kiss. "I've wanted you in my bed from the first moment I saw you. My brother's a fool to turn you away." He leaned in again running his lips along her cheek and pulling in a deep breath—scenting her. She recognized it from all the times Lucian had done it, and it sent a horrifying flush of remembered lust through her. But this was the wrong brother. This was all wrong.

"Let me show you what real dragon love can feel like." He was still breathing words into her ear. "I can taste your need, your desire, Arabella. Let me make you scream my name while I make you mine."

But that word—*love*—was what finally broke the spell. *Yes*, Leonidas was every inch a gorgeous dragon shifter, as much as, possibly more than, his brother. But what she felt for Lucian wasn't mere lust—there was a kindness in his heart, a brokenness and darkness that needed her. And she couldn't imagine in a million years if their positions were reversed, that Lucian would ever go after the woman that Leonidas had just slept with… even if he had rejected her and told her to leave.

When she pushed Leonidas away this time, she meant it. His eyes went a little wide, and he eased back to give her room.

She curled her lip in disgust. "How can you do such an awful thing? He's your brother, Leonidas!"

This time, his smile was all smirk and no seduction. "A treasure so easily won would not have been worthy of my brother."

What? Was this some kind of game? *Fuck.* "You're an ass! I'm going to tell him." The heat of shame and embarrassment washed through her, making her angry.

Leonidas leaned back and wiped the wetness of her kiss from his lips. "Please do. He'll thank me."

The coolness of his voice infuriated her. *Fucking dragons.* Was she just a plaything for them? "No, he won't!" But then all her doubts flooded back.

"Well," he said, his smirk growing stronger. *"Thank you* might be a bit of an exaggeration. He'll try to kill me first. Probably burn a few holes in my hide. But it will be worth it." The smirk faded from his face. "An unworthy mate for Lucian is something I would happily die to prevent from happening again."

Her jealousy and anger and shame evaporated. She squinted at him, remembering the reason she was here in the first place. *Information.* "You mean his previous mate."

Leonidas's eyes went cold. "It wasn't carrying a dragonling that killed Cara."

Cara? Lucian had never mentioned her name.

"Her love for him wasn't True," Leonidas added. He nailed her with those sapphire blue eyes. "I had to see, little Arabella, if you were just hot for my brother's bed, and any dragon would do, or if you truly thought you were in love. Because it will break Lucian if your love isn't True, and I simply won't allow that to happen."

A surge of excitement made her step forward and lift her chin. "I *am* in love with him. I have no idea how to tell if it's a True Love or not, but I know this—I don't know anywhere near what I need to know to figure it out. And all of this is related to a treaty no one will explain to me. *That's* why I'm here. You need to tell me, Leonidas. If you care about Lucian the way you claim…" She dared him with her eyes. "The way *I* do… then you'll tell me what I need to know."

The man actually took a step back and regarded her as if she had transformed into a strange magical beast in front of his eyes. "You really mean that." He said it like he was stunned.

She balled up her fists. "I need to know the truth, Leonidas—I'm a lawyer, for fuck's sake. Show me the treaty. Let me read it. Let me figure this thing out."

His eyebrows went up first, then he gave a dry laugh. "It's in dragontongue, Bella dear. Every dragon is born knowing how to read it, but it would be indecipherable to you."

"Then tell me what it says." *Asshole.* She left that part unspoken because she was finally close to getting some real answers.

He examined her for a beat, then two, and slowly nodded. "All right, little human. I'll tell you all the secrets of the House of Smoke and the fae realm and every other small and terribly horrible thing that you really don't want to know... if you make me a promise."

"What promise?" Negotiations, good. This was *her* realm.

"That if you can't truly love my brother—if you have even the slightest, tiny doubt—that you will leave. Leave the keep. Leave my brother. And never come back."

"Deal." She lifted her chin. "If I can't love your brother, I have no reason to be here."

He narrowed his eyes but nodded. Then he gestured for her to come in the rest of the way to his lair, bringing her to his beautifully appointed great room with the bright white leather couch. He indicated that she sit, and she did, but her body was a live wire of energy waiting to hear what he had to say.

He took a seat next to her. "To understand the treaty, you need to know how it came about."

She nodded.

"The Winter and Summer fae draw from the two poles of energy," Leonidas said, draping his arm across the back of the couch, looking substantially more relaxed. "The Winter fae are pretty much assholes, predictably cold and very erratic. The Summer fae are no less strange, but they tend to be warmer and more... *passionate.* Ten thousand years ago, the Summer Queen, like many queens before her, had many lovers. There was only one king, mind you, a true fae who could give her pure fae children. But this Summer Queen broke the one and only rule among their kind... she fell in love with one of her lovers."

"Sounds like a lot of drama for drawing up a treaty." Arabella hope she was getting the truth from Leonidas, and this wasn't some kind of game he was playing with her. *Again.*

"Patience," he said with a smile. "As I said, you need to understand how it came about."

She waved for him to hurry it up.

"The Queen of the Summer Court fell in love with a dragon." He dipped his chin and stared at her with his beautiful blue eyes, giving her that same sultry smirk that he had lavished on her by the door. "Perhaps you can imagine how that might've happened?"

She definitely could. Her face heated up with remembered shame, but she pushed through it. "Seducing a human is one thing. Seducing a Fae Queen must've been an altogether more difficult task."

Leonidas broke out into a broad grin, and he gave a half laugh. "I can see why Lucian can't seem to let you go."

That made her blush in an entirely different way. "Get on with it." She scowled to try to bring back the seriousness. And to wipe away the heat on her face. "We don't have time to mess around. You didn't see Lucian in my apartment. He almost turned into…"

Leonidas's smile fled, and a frown crashed down on his face. "Turned into what?"

She shook her head. "I don't know. He wouldn't explain it. Cinaed refused to say a word. But Lucian was losing control. Like his dragon was taking over."

Leonidas's face opened in surprise. Then he rubbed both hands across his face, scrubbing it. He looked back to her. "But he contained it, right?"

She nodded, lips pursed tight.

He shook his head and stared at the couch between them for a moment. "Fuck," he said softly. "I thought for sure we had more time."

"More time for what?" she demanded, peering at him. "I need to know, Leonidas."

He nodded and looked at her thoughtfully. "That was his *wyvern* form. It's an animal—a wild animal, Arabella. It is the end of his human life. A form of evolution, I suppose, but if a dragon doesn't take a mate and successfully spawn a drag-onling, that is what he will turn into."

She drew back. "So that's what Lucian meant when he said the clock was ticking for him. That he would die."

He nodded. "That is true for every dragon, but my brother carries the additional burden of the treaty."

"Tell me." She gave him her most determined look.

He pulled in a breath and continued. "The

Queen of the Summer Court fell in love with her dragon lover, and she bore him a child. A child conceived of love and magic—half dragon and half fae. Only the King of the Summer Court, the fae husband, found out. Apparently, it is one thing to have a lover, and another thing entirely to bring children into the world from that coupling—something that only could have been done voluntarily. Apparently, the fae do not accidentally get pregnant, not unlike dragons. You cannot imagine the wrath of that fae husband. The magic they have, Arabella, is like nothing you've ever seen. The world literally shook."

She just nodded for him to keep going.

"The queen made a magical vow to protect her lover and their child and all of humanity from the wrath of the fae. She foresaw that she would have to protect her dragon children in perpetuity, or her husband would find a way around the binding magic and eventually kill her progeny. She sealed it with her love, and it was given further power by her death at the hands of her husband. When the magical smoke cleared, her fae children could not believe they were bound by a magical vow their mother had made… all to serve their bastard half-brother and their mother's promise to her lover. It was a wonder that dragonkind survived at all—indeed, a great many Houses perished in the subsequent wrath. The House of Smoke alone was untouchable, and they sheltered many of the other Houses from the fae husband. Eventually, the King of the Summer Court had finished venting his wrath. Passions cooled, and the conditions of the vow were made clear."

"Is this vow the same as the treaty?" Her eyes were wide, taking this all in.

"Nearly so. The treaty is an agreement between the Summer and Winter Courts to abide by the conditions of the magical vow the queen made in her death throes. It keeps them from war over it. The vow says that as long as a child of the House of Smoke lives, no fae may kill any dragon whose lineage traces back to the Summer Queen. As a safeguard to allow the House of Smoke to continue to propagate, she included the protection of humanity under her vow, as all human females were potential mates and would be necessary to the continuation of the House."

"So that's how the treaty protects humans—it prevents the fae from harming us so we can mate with dragons." Her mind was spinning with all this. From what little she knew of the fae, in her encounter with a prince of the Winter Court, that protection was vital. She couldn't even imagine what the world would suddenly be like if the fae were able to mess with humans whenever they liked.

"Yes. Specifically, so you can mate with the House of Smoke. Very specifically, with the crown prince."

"Lucian." It really *did* all come down to him.

Leonidas nodded solemnly. "This treaty was made when humanity was just a small tribe wandering the grasslands in Africa. The dragons had been mating with them for millennia, depending on them to perpetuate their species. The queen needed to ensure that that small population would continue—otherwise, the fae could simply wipe out humanity and by extension wipe out dragonkind. Of course, she could not possibly have imagined the evolution of the human race into its current form. But you're still just as vulnerable to the fae as you were when you were scrabbling around, learning how to plant wheat and gather berries."

"So if Lucian doesn't have a dragonling... why can't you or Lucian's other brother—Leksander— fulfill the treaty?" This seemed overly restrictive to her. Especially considering the fate of humanity rested on it.

"Well, the fae are very particular about their treaties and the exact wording of them. It's difficult to translate the original dragontongue, but it essentially says, "the first surviving spawn" of the King and Queen of the House of Smoke that carries fae blood. And that's Lucian. Triplets are so incredibly unusual among dragonkind, there's no real specification for it in the treaty. Normally, there is only a single dragonling. And since Lucian lived, and was the first dragonling to do so, he fulfills the treaty. Which is a good thing, because I managed to fuck up my chances to ever truly mate long ago."

She frowned. "What did you do?"

He shook his head and waved it off. "It involves a witch, a curse, and a lot of sex. And it's a story for another day. What you need to know, Arabella Sharp, is that the treaty very specifically says that, not only does the House of Smoke have to propagate its line, but that any female who mates with the dragon prince from the House of Smoke must truly be in love with her dragon. The Fae Queen's vow was born of love—a True Love that transcended the differences between fae and dragon, and even transcended death. That's powerful magic, and it's encoded in the vow and the treaty. There can be no doubt about this love."

Arabella nodded. "It has to be a True Love. That's what Lucian said."

"Yes. And you, Arabella, will not survive the sealing and the bearing of a dragonling unless your love is True. I believe that's what killed Cara—a moment of doubt is all it takes. It's one reason why the drive to procreate is so strong among dragons. Because we must try again and again and again."

She swallowed, the horror of that sinking in.

"Is that really what you want to sign up for?" he asked pointedly.

She just frowned. How would she ever know for sure that her love was True? "I don't understand— isn't it natural for there to be some doubt in how much you love someone?" Not that she really knew anything about love. That much was clear from every relationship she had ever had. At least, prior to Lucian. She was in completely uncharted territory with him.

Leonidas shrugged. "I'm sure I wouldn't know. I haven't ever been in love, personally."

She raised her eyebrows. "Never?"

He waved it off again. "What matters is this— only True Love will make the treaty work. Only

True Love will keep the realms apart. Only True Love will allow you to survive this, Arabella. If you're not the woman for this, stand aside. Let Lucian find someone who is."

A horrible squeezing feeling pressed down on her chest. She didn't know what to say to that, so she just nodded and rose up from the couch.

Leonidas watched her carefully.

"Thank you," she mumbled. "Thank you for being honest with me." She turned and hurried toward the front door, letting herself out. Leonidas didn't follow. She wanted to believe he was lying to her, but she didn't. Every word he said had the ring of truth to it.

Only True Love will allow you to survive…

But how would she ever know?

Chapter Five

WHEN LUCIAN FINALLY AROSE OUT OF THE darkness of sleep, he felt drugged.

He had slept so hard and so long that it was almost as dark in his room as it had been in his unconscious state. He groggily flicked a small spell at the screen opposite his bed, and the clock was summoned. It was well into the evening, nearing 10 o'clock, but he had no sense of the passage of time —he had to check the date even to see what day it was. It was still the same one, just nearing the end of it. But he was no longer in danger of losing control and turning wyvern.

Thank magic for that.

Thoughts of almost losing control made him reflexively reach out with his fae senses and search the keep for Arabella. She was still in her apartment, something that churned both frustration and pride through him. She'd seen him nearly become a beast she surely did not recognize, and yet she was still here. He had ordered her away—nay *begged* her to leave—and yet she was still here. And even across the stretch of the keep, the touch of her scent on his mind and the refreshment of sleep aroused him, springing his cock to life.

Fuck. That was the last thing he needed.

He dragged himself out of the warm embrace of the sheets and headed for the shower. He magically dispensed with his clothing and stepped into the cool water, letting it cascade down his body and hoping it would cool off the raging hard-on that even the mere scent of her had given him. It wasn't working, and he contemplated giving himself some release. Even as his hand stroked his cock to make quick work of it, prudence held him back. The solution was not to get off with dreams of Arabella in his head. What he needed was to take his release with another woman. Again and again and again… until he forgot the sweet taste of Arabella's scent.

As if forgetting was something he knew how to do.

He shut off the cold water and stepped from the

shower, toweling off. He would need all the residual lust heat that he could muster to accomplish this. Finding a woman to bury himself in, much less seducing her and carrying out his duty, would take all the willpower he had. Possibly more. He gritted his teeth, determined in this vile task, not because it was what he wanted. Not even because it was an honorable thing to do, at least, not for the woman involved. Only because it was his duty, which the fate of humanity rested upon.

He conjured a tailored suit, trim and draped across his body in the current fashion. It was hunting gear, the kind he saw Leonidas wearing lately—the kind that aroused women.

Then Lucian searched for his phone and swiped open the app—WildLove—that Arabella had taught him how to use. It was simple, easy, and far faster than hunting through the human bars, as his brother did. Then again, Leonidas didn't have to accomplish the same purpose. Lucian swiped through the candidates—there was a seemingly endless supply of them. He was looking for certain characteristics. Most definitely not green eyes, but something that showed a glimmer of the strength this woman would need to endure being his mate. He would have to meet them personally—very personally—and taste them to see if they had anywhere near the strength of Arabella. Or any chance of surviving at all. And they would need more than that—they would need the capacity for True Love, something that perhaps was even more rare. He set up a dozen liaisons, each at the same hotel in downtown Seattle that he had used before for his ill-fated "date." With that one, he had never intended to carry through—it had been just a ruse to arouse jealousy in his real target, Arabella. And he'd succeeded all too well in that endeavor, losing his heart as well.

There would be no chance of that this time. His heart already belonged to her.

As the messages flooded in, these women all hot and ready for sex, he queued them up fifteen minutes apart. Speed dating for a mate, he supposed. But he should know with the first taste if they were right for the job. If not, then he could hustle them out the door before the next arrived. And the unluckiest one of all, he would take to bed right away. This time, he would start the seduction immediately with an orgasm. This was business, nothing more, and he needed to do it right. Maybe if he had had such sense about him before, he wouldn't have fallen in love with Arabella in the first place.

He took the stairwell to the roof from his own lair, not wanting to chance meeting anyone in the halls of the keep, especially his brothers. They'd made their opinions abundantly clear—he should send Arabella away. And while he may not be capable of that—indeed, had already reached the limits of what he was able to do in begging her to leave—if he returned with another woman and took her obviously to his bed, perhaps that would finally send Arabella packing. In fact, her anger at him might be just the shield he needed to keep from running back into her arms with the slightest look or touch.

The flight from the keep to Seattle was short. When he had landed, decloaked, and re-dressed himself in his seductive evening attire, he strode into the hotel. He had arrived mere minutes before the first prospect was to show up at the door to his room.

Even so, he paced every inch of the expansive hotel suite he had acquired for the night, feeling every second of the waiting time crawl up his back. It was like a demon that dug deeper and deeper into his soul with every step. He had to remind himself over and over again, like a chant, that this was his duty. Did every crown prince of the House of Smoke endure this agony? Would this always be the fate of his House and his family to have to succumb to the demands of the treaty? His mother had a True Love for his father by necessity, but it was obvious that his father adored his mother as well—his gaze, even now in their old age, never strayed far from her, and they sported a vigorous and resplendent love that was clear to all. But they were both dragon, something extremely rare—as rare as the triplets they bore from their love.

Lucian imagined the original love between the Fae Queen and her dragon lover was similarly transcendent. And no prince of the House of Smoke had ever, in the ten thousand years since, failed in his duty to win the love of a human woman to bear his dragonling. Less clear was how many had truly loved the woman who bore them a son. If Lucian failed to produce a dragonling, he would be the first... and he would be jeopardizing all of humanity with it. But he would also end the torment, once and for all, and not only for himself, but for his House.

He snorted in disgust. That was one of the most

self-serving thoughts he had ever had, and it was no credit to him that he'd had it several times before.

A knock at the door summoned him. He straightened his shoulders, wiped the self-pity from his mind, and strode toward it.

The first candidate was a gorgeous, well-built blonde. However, even with the door just barely open, and before she could speak, he could tell she was vapid and spoilt. She tasted of self-indulgence. The surface sexuality that was rampant across her body and throughout her scent said she took her pleasure from many men but worried not about the pleasure she gave in return. Her body was barely concealed in a clingy silk dress—it was intended as a lure and not any bold proclamation of her strength or sexuality.

"Are you Lucian Smoke?" she asked with a smile that revealed gleaming white, perfectly straight teeth behind her bright red lipstick.

"Sorry, you have the wrong room." Lucian closed the door in her face.

He shouldn't take satisfaction from that action, but he did. As he paced away from the door, the curses in the hallway could be heard even without his enhanced dragon senses. He made the circuit around his hotel room suite, past the grand, king-size bed, along the two-story wall of windows looking out over Seattle's downtown, past the small living room area with the crackling fireplace, and back to the door again. He would keep the pacing up until the next one arrived; with any luck, the first one would be gone by then. If not, then that confrontation would be illuminating, if nothing else.

Agitation continued to itch its way up his back as he waited, but he was more determined in his purpose now. When the second knock came, he was ready.

This time, he reached out before he opened the door, tasting her with his fae senses. This one had an electric strength in her, snapping and buzzing with energy. It came not from darkness, but from a raw, almost brutal nature. She was a fighter with an ornery nature, and she had had many conquests in bed. Lucian would merely be her latest.

He opened the door, and she looked just like her image on WildLove—fiery blue eyes, blazing red hair. She had a ghost of freckles across her cheeks, a thought that Lucian shoved roughly to the side. There would be no comparisons to Arabella tonight.

"Damn," she said, looking him up and down. "You're even hotter in person."

"Are you sure?" he asked, giving her the half smile he knew reached inside a woman and dialed up her arousal. Although her scent was already filling his senses. "Perhaps you should take a taste to be sure." He stepped back to give her room to come in.

Her eyes lit up, and a hungry smile took over her face. She marched in and slammed the door behind her, then she was on him, hands grabbing at his shoulders and his hair, lips crashing against his. She practically climbed him, hooking her long leg over his hip and grinding her body against him. He grabbed hold of her ass and pulled her tighter, willing his cock to stiffen and show her that he returned her raging lust, even if it weren't true. She ground and ground against him, helping with that cause. Her tongue was plundering his mouth, and his was in return. He could have hot, angry sex with her, no question. They could fuck until dawn, ravaging each other's bodies… but under the harshness, the brutal strength of this woman, there was no inner softness.

She snaked a hand down between them and grabbed his cock through his clothes, giving it a swift stroke. His body responded, growing harder in her grasp, but inside he was already deciding her fate.

Lucky for her, it wouldn't involve spending the night in his bed.

He reached down and grasped her hand away from his cock, and said, "I'm sorry. You have to leave."

"What?" It wasn't a question filled with disbelief —she seemed to think she had misheard him.

He grabbed both of her wrists and held them wide apart, then stepped back from her, holding her body away from his, just make himself absolutely clear. "I changed my mind. Leave now."

The proud strength of her face went through a convoluted shifting of emotions—first disbelief, then horror, then a raging-hot anger. She struggled in his hold, trying to break free, no doubt to take a swing at him. When that proved unsuccessful, her knee came up. He released her hand to catch her leg and gently shove it aside.

"You asshole!" she said, but she was backing away, the red of her anger coloring her face and spitting out in her words.

She would never know that she should thank him. But she didn't have the capacity to be what he needed. There was no soft love waiting to be revealed under that hard, brittle exterior. He could seduce her—and he had no doubt the sex would be satisfying if nothing else—but she was not the kind to fall in love, least of all with a man like him, no matter how soft his charms. She would leave him, or more likely, never agree to something like the sealing in the first place.

"I'm sure you'll find someone else willing to spread your legs," he said, letting disdain drip into his voice. It was a horrible thing to say—and probably the only thing that would drive her from the room without him having to physically throw her out.

A shrill growl rumbled in her chest, and her fists clenched at her sides. "I don't have to take this shit from you!"

He gestured to the door. No, she didn't—*she really didn't*—and he desperately hoped she would take that insult and leave.

Thanks be to magic, she did.

She slammed open the hotel door on her way, leaving it gaping. She stormed down the hall, her growl of anger still trailing after her along with the stomp of her high-heeled shoes.

Lucian dragged himself to the door, then slowly and quietly closed it. He braced both hands against it and banged his head on the stained oak. *For the love of magic.* Only two, and he was already worn out. Tarnished deep in his soul with this sordid business. How the fuck was he going to endure this? How had the other dragons before him managed it?

Not for the first time, he wondered if his ancestors were all brutal rapists. Like Tytus, the black dragon, who took his pleasure from hunting women like prey. But no… somehow they had won the love of their humans—True Love, indeed—but those were different times. Times when women expected less of a man but deserved even more for all they suffered. Somehow, the dragons before him had done it. Maybe they were not as soft of heart as Lucian was. It was the only answer that he could draw upon that made any sense—that *he* was the problem, not the treaty.

He must've been standing at the door for a long time, his head resting wearily against it, as the next knock took him by surprise. He jerked away from the door and stumbled two steps back, eyeing it warily. Then he reached forward with his fae senses to get a heads up on this one.

She was different.

This one tasted of a deep, dark hurt, and a long-suffering, aching need for love. She had been hurt too many times, and now she was showing up at his door because she believed she was good for nothing else. Good for only this. For sex. With a stranger. This night would be something to ease the ache in her body even though she was convinced that the ache in her heart was a permanent stain.

She was perfect.

He pulled open the door. "Hello," he said, keeping his voice soft and inviting. "You can't possibly be the woman from the WildLove app, can you?" He made an obvious effort of looking her up and down, checking her out. She was tremendously beautiful—long brown hair, deep brown eyes. Luminous skin, pale. "It can't be that I have found such a treasure simply through an app."

A delicate blush graced her face. He had to wonder at all the horribles that must've happened to her to have a compliment be so rare that it still brought a blush to her face.

"Well, I could say the same about you." She swallowed and seemed to be embarrassed about sneaking looks at his body.

He stepped back. "Please come in."

She stepped inside, and he quietly closed the door behind her. With a sweep of his arm, he invited her deeper into the hotel suite, avoiding the bed and shepherding her toward the less intimidating couch in the center of the living area, in front of the fireplace.

"Please have a seat."

She did, looking up at him with those wide brown eyes.

He had no idea who this woman was, but that innocent look speared guilt through him, regardless. She didn't know the danger she was walking into. And he could tell she was already halfway to being seduced without him even trying.

He sat beside her, deliberately letting his leg casually brush against hers and then pulling back. She seemed to be steeling herself not to flinch away. He draped his arm across the back of the couch, not touching her but coming close.

"What's your name?" he asked.

"Rebecca?" She looked at him a little oddly like he should've known that.

And he should have... only he had gone through a hundred choices before settling on the dozen meetups, and he hadn't kept track of their names.

"Is that your real name?" he asked, hopefully covering for his mistake. "No one seems to use their real names on the app."

"Oh!" That delicate flush came to her face again. "I didn't realize…" She dropped her gaze, flitting it across the couch between them. "This is my first time. I didn't know I wasn't supposed to use my real name. I guess I should've known that."

He reached for her chin with his finger and gently lifted it up so that she would have to look him in the eyes. "Don't be embarrassed. This is my first time, too." What was one more lie among many?

"Really?" she asked. He could feel her naiveté like a bitter sweetness. Her gullibility was another stab through his heart.

"Yes, but I have a feeling it's going to be my last." He brushed the back of his hand up her cheek, and her lips parted. He slipped his hand into her hair and gently pulled her toward him as he leaned in for the kiss. He kept it soft and hesitant at first, then a little stronger. She came alive in his arms, her hands skimming featherlight across his shoulders and into his hair as if she didn't know quite what to do with them.

She was delicious, and he could feel her opening up to him like a fresh, new flower.

She was the one.

He could have sex with her and have her falling in love with him before dawn. And it was a certainty that he wouldn't fall in love with her—partly because he was already in love with Arabella, and partly because seducing this woman was like crushing a kitten. He was dragging her into a fate she didn't expect nor deserve.

He deepened his kiss, exploring her mouth with his tongue, and dropping his hand to caress her breast. She moaned, and her breathing hitched. Her arousal perfumed the air and stiffened his cock. He would have no trouble having sex with her—she was just the kind his body responded to, soft and sweet and hungry—but this would be all about her pleasure, not his. He could already tell that on the first orgasm, he would have her heart. Then he would have to set about repairing the darkness and damage deep inside her by lavishing her with praise and sweet concern.

Even as he leaned her back on the couch, covering her with his body and grinding his cock against her, to let her know he desired her as well, he couldn't help thinking how different she was from Arabella. This woman had been defeated by her darkness, and she would need Lucian to save her from it. But Arabella... she'd already rescued herself. He had only to remind her body that it could love again, that was all. The rest had been just a repeat of that reminder, again and again, causing her to open up to him a little more each time and paving the way for the full reclaiming of her own self. For Arabella, he was merely the key that unlocked her ability to completely heal herself. She was the one who opened the door and did the work. She was already a master at taking darkness and turning it into light. She did it every day with others… she only needed a reminder of how to do it with herself.

The body underneath him writhed and bucked. He dropped his lips to her neck, tasting her there and burying his face in her billow of brown hair.

"You like that?" he asked, his voice soft and seductive in her ear, as he let his hands travel down and feel every curve of her body.

"Oh God," she breathed.

His hand slipped down into the front of her pants, finding her sex already dripping wet.

"Oh God, oh God, oh God," she panted.

He worked her sex with one hand, using the other to weave into her hair and hold her tight. He needed to keep her still as she squirmed underneath him so that he could wrench pleasure out of her softness with his strength. He was already envisioning himself buried in her, the soft sweep of her hair against his face as he gripped her sweet flesh in his hands.

He nibbled at her neck and whispered in her ear, "Do you want more?"

"Oh yes." She moaned and bucked again as he worked her sex even harder.

A haze was drawing over his mind. The power of her ache, her need, was flooding his mind. His thoughts cast back to that blessedly endless time when he had Arabella in his bed. Making her come the first time, and the tenth, and the twentieth after that. It was a haze of lust and love and sex, touching and loving, building and falling on great waves of pure pleasure. "Oh, how I'm going to make you come, my sweet Arabella…"

She and he both froze with his words.

A shock of horror ripped through him. He stilled the motion of his hand working her body. Then he pulled his hand away.

"Who is Arabella?" The woman asked, but she was already scrambling back on the couch to get away from him.

He squeezed his eyes shut, grimaced. *Fuck.* How far gone was he that he had allowed that to happen? He just shook his head and opened his eyes. Small tears were trickling lines down Rebecca's face.

"Oh God," she said, only this time it was filled with fear. "You're going to hurt me, aren't you?"

Guilt speared through him again for giving her even that small measure of fear, but the truth was that she was lucky—she was escaping a fate worse than she knew. "You should leave."

Her eyes went even wider, and she started trembling, but she scrambled off the couch and tugged hastily at her clothes to straighten them. She was shaking and crying and made to bolt toward the door. He caught her wrist to stop her as she tried to fly past him. At least he could undo some of the damage he'd already done in mere moments with her.

"It's not you, Rebecca. It's definitely me. Everything I said was true. You're beautiful and sexy, and any man would be lucky to have your heart. Please try again. With someone who isn't broken, like me."

He released her, but his words didn't seem to ease her panic. She fled for the door, hurrying out of it and pulling it shut behind her.

Lucian leaned forward, bracing his elbows on his knees and dropping his head into his hands. *Fuck,* he'd screwed that up, but good. And he had been thoroughly deluding himself about this working. *Goddammit.* He had been thinking about Arabella the entire time while taking this woman's clothes off. Those weren't Rebecca's breasts he was fondling, they were Arabella's. *Fuck.* And now that he was out of that delusional haze of lust, his inner dragon was disgusted by what he had done.

This woman—Rebecca—was exactly the type that Lucian needed to fulfill his duty, but she wasn't even close to what his dragon wanted. *Only Arabella would do,* whether she was even in the room or not. Lucian angrily stood and paced the room again, glancing at the clock to see when the next woman was to arrive. But a creeping horror seeped into him—he wasn't going to find anyone who would be more perfect for seduction than Rebecca, and he hadn't even come close to executing on it. The only reason his dragon had gone along at all with the charade was because his thoughts were drenched in Arabella.

Because he'd already shed blood for her. *Already* risked everything for her.

And his dragon had made the decision for him —*she* was his mate, and no other would do.

The despair of that carved deep into him, and he felt the wildness of his wyvern stir in his blood. It wanted out. Wanted to find her and claim her. His beast wanted to seal her against her will, plant his seed in her, spawn a dragonling, all of it. That was the price of reaching this stage without mating—his instincts were kicking in, his animal nature taking over as a matter of survival. Whether Lucian liked it or not, his dragon would revert to a brutal animal and claim his mate—in a rape that was designed to impregnate and procreate and extend his life.

He couldn't do that to Arabella, for fuck's sake.

He would sooner slit his own throat.

That was it—he would have to sequester himself, allow himself to go wyvern in some place where he would be trapped or killed. Under no circumstances could his wyvern be allowed to reach her. Because it was clear, there would be no other woman for him.

Humanity would be damned, but he would *not* let her be the first casualty.

Lucian strode out of the hotel suite, leaving the door ajar and not looking back.

Chapter Six

"Please tell me you did not actually sleep with my best friend."

Arabella kept her voice low so that Rachel wouldn't hear her from across the pool room. She had just dived into the water and was paddling around.

"I already told you, my lady," Cinaed said roughly, keeping his voice down as well. "I did not bed your best friend in the very short time during which you were gone. Mind you, it wasn't for lack of desire on her part." He was pissed that she kept asking, but she still wasn't quite sure she believed him. Especially with the way his eyes tracked Rachel's every movement in her skimpy bikini—the one that Cinaed had conjured for her. Arabella was wearing one just as revealing, but somehow Cinaed only had eyes for Rachel's curves.

"Just keep it that way, all right?" Of course, she had used Rachel to distract Cinaed, but that was as far as she wanted it to go. Things would get seriously messy if Rachel were entangled with Cinaed. And Arabella's mind was already a mess as it was.

"Aye, my lady. I keep my promises." But he was biting his lip as Rachel climbed out of the pool, dripping wet. "She's not the kind for me, in any event."

That ruffled Arabella's feathers. But then again she was on edge already. "What are you saying? My best friend is awesome, and anyone that says otherwise is a damn liar."

His eyebrows rose. "Awesome? If by that you mean tremendously good at being quarrelsome and ornery and sharp-tongued…" He faded off as Rachel approached. He blinked and seemed to be struggling to keep his eyes off Rachel's chest, which was barely concealed by the thin green stretch of triangular fabric trying to contain her ample breasts. Arabella didn't know what he expected, but perhaps Rachel's nipples standing at attention due to the chill of the pool room after climbing out of the warm water wasn't exactly it. Rachel had a

ALISA WOODS

towel, and Arabella was sure her best friend knew exactly the picture she was presenting because she sure as hell wasn't using that towel to cover up anything.

Cinaed's lips were parted, and Arabella wouldn't be surprised to see drool dribbling down his chin.

Rachel looked Cinaed up and down—he was likewise in a swimsuit but had declined to join them in the pool. Then she flicked a look to Arabella. "What are you talking about?" she asked, suspicious. As if she didn't know they were talking about her. Rachel was too savvy for that—she was just trying to bait Cinaed.

"Just what I should do about Lucian," Arabella said, trying to steer clear of the high-voltage tension that was still bouncing between the two of them.

Rachel scowled. "Well, I told you—fuck that guy!"

Mission accomplished in the distraction department, Arabella thought, wryly. But that wasn't exactly the answer she wanted. She had been struggling all day with what to do and getting no closer to an answer. After talking to Leonidas, she'd come back to the apartment and argued with Rachel about this whole situation—the treaty, True Love, whether Arabella had any chance with Lucian after he had pushed her away so many times, and the whole tragic nature of his situation, now that she understood it. But Rachel was having none of it. And had loudly said so. Repeatedly.

Arabella had wanted to go immediately and talk to Lucian, but Cinaed had told her the truth about his endless patrols, so she knew he was exhausted. He needed time to rest and to think, and supposedly, he had gone to his lair to sleep. So she waited… and waited… and when she couldn't wait anymore, she worked up the courage to go talk to him… and he wasn't even there. He had left the keep. With a little probing, she found out he had gone to the city. She couldn't believe he was hunting demons again so soon, and just on a lark, she decided to check his WildLove app. She still had the login. Sure enough, he'd lined up a dozen women to have hookups with that night.

When Rachel had seen it, she'd gone ballistic.

Arabella sighed. "I know you think I should just give up, Rach—"

"*Ari!*" she cut her off. "He's off *fucking other women.* What else do you need to know?" She threw a glare at Cinaed.

He cringed and didn't say anything. Which

really should tell her everything she needed to know, if even Cinaed thought it was hopeless. Rachel turned back to her. "Not that this place isn't like a glorious five-star hotel, but I'm ready to leave at any time. Midnight swims are awesome…" She gestured at the sparkling moonlit landscape outside the windows of the pool room. "But you don't need this hot mess of trouble."

She was right—Arabella didn't need the trouble. But it wasn't just her life, or even her love life, at stake here. "This is about more than just me, Rach. This is kind of save-the-world time."

"*Pft.*" Rachel stuck out her tongue. "Let someone else save the world. Besides, you don't know that brother of his isn't making all this shit up. How much of this treaty business do you *really* know is true?"

"I saw the fae for myself," she pointed out.

Cinaed was back to just shaking his head as if Rachel were ridiculously clueless. To be fair, her best friend had only just learned about dragon shifters and demons and the fae this morning. It was entirely reasonable for any person to be doubting at this point. Doubly so for Rachel, who was a natural doubter.

"Prince Zephan is real," Arabella said. "The fae

are real. And they're definitely not people you want messing with humanity. Which Prince Zephan would do just for shits and giggles, because that guy's an asshole. He makes your exes look like sweethearts. Never mind if he actually had a *reason* to mess with humans, which he very well might, given that we are part of this treaty thing. This is a real problem, Rach."

"Aye," Cinaed agreed a little too eagerly. "And my lady is the only one I've seen have an impact on my prince in a long, long time."

Arabella raised her eyebrows at that new piece of information. Once Leonidas had broken the shroud of secrecy around all this, Cinaed seemed to think that liberated him from his vow of silence. Or maybe it was seeing Lucian nearly turn into his wyvern form. That had freaked him out as much as it had Leonidas.

"Hey, McHottie," Rachel said with bite in her voice. "You don't get a vote on this."

"Well, I should," he threw back, his eyes finally locked on her face and not her chest. "It's clear neither of you understands a thing about love."

Arabella grimaced. "Well, he's right about that." How would she even know she was in love? Much less True Love?

"Hey, fuck you," Rachel said to Cinaed. He rolled his eyes and threw up his hands like he wasn't sure why he even bothered to try. Rachel turned back to her. "Seriously, Arabella, do you even hear yourself? Lucian's off with other women. He is *banging* them as we speak. And you still want him? Sister, that's not love. That's sickness and obsession. Codependent bullshit. You know this."

She wasn't wrong about that. In fact, those were the exact words that kept cycling through Arabella's mind every time she tried to tease out all the pieces of this big hairy mess.

"I know," Arabella said. "And yet…"

Rachel gave a noise of disgust and crossed her arms. "There is no *and yet* in this. Just a whole lot of *Nope.*"

"All I know is that everything you've said is true… and yet, I still want to be with him. More importantly, I really believe I'm the one to heal his heart, which is what he's going to need to mate and have a chance at making a dragonling. How can I believe that so strongly, if it isn't true? How can I have this delusional belief that I'm the one to fulfill this grand treaty?" She was waving her hands around and doubting it all over again, now that she was saying it out loud. "It all sounds crazy. And yet… you should've seen the way he looks at me…"

Before Rachel could open her mouth in protest again, Cinaed took a step forward, coming between the two of them. He looked Arabella square in the eyes. "What is love but obsession with another person more than anything else in this world? What is love but a sickness in your heart when the other is gone?"

Rachel muscled her way forward, shoving on Cinaed with his big bulky muscles as if she could physically push him off to the side. "What do you know about love, McHottie?"

This brought the red up to his face in an instant. He turned and glared down at her shorter form. She crossed her arms and stood staring up at him, dressed in nothing but her wet bikini and her defiant stare. Arabella held back her smirk. She was absolutely sure they were loathing each other right now—and just as sure that if she let Cinaed off the leash, they would be locking lips and other parts very shortly. The sizzle was red-hot between them.

"I know it because it was *taken* from me." Cinaed's words held such passion that they wiped the smirk off Arabella's face. Her heart stood still, listening for more. "I know it because I had it

ripped from my life when I was just a young dragonling. It was taken from my father, who loved my
mother and raged against the brutal men who took
her from him. Those same men took them both
from me. I don't believe in love because it's a
figment of my imagination—the whole treaty was
built on the idea of True Love. It's a magic that
plainly exists for anyone with eyes to see. It is as real
as the magic I breathe from my lips." He turned,
pulled in a breath, and blew dragonfire across the
pool. It curled blue flames that roiled and boiled the
water wherever it touched, then dissipated into mist.

Arabella stood stock still, not breathing. Even
Rachel look stunned—not so much for the magical
display, but the passion and the deepness of the
hurt behind it.

Cinaed turned back to them, his face full of
grief and anger for the loved ones he lost. "And I
feel sorry for anyone who doesn't believe in the
magic of love." He gave Rachel a scorching look,
and for once she had no retort. She just stood there
for a moment with her mouth hanging open.

The air grew thick with the tension between
them. They were either going to kiss or—

"Hey, why don't you just fuck off?" Rachel said,
taking a step back and scowling.

Or fight.

"Don't tempt me, woman." He looked like he might grab her and throw her in the pool. Or kiss her. Damn, it was hard to tell with these two.

Rachel scowled. "What the hell does that even *mean?*"

"Hello? Remember me?" Arabella butted into their obsession with each other. She didn't want them sleeping together, but she wasn't sure fighting was any better. "We're talking about my problems? Oh, and the fate of humanity?"

Cinaed pulled back from his anger a little quicker than Rachel, but Arabella had managed to grab both their attention again.

She dropped the sarcasm from her voice. "Cinaed, I'm sorry about what happened to your parents. And I don't know if I believe in this True Love thing, but all of you do. The fae do. Dragons do. It has to be real, and I know it's important. But I've only got one chance to try to do this again. I might not even have that. It might already be too late. And now that I really know the stakes… this is just too important to let go."

"My lady," he said, his voice solemn. "If there's anyone who can do this, it's you."

She nodded. "I suppose. Maybe. But if it's

ALISA WOODS

possible… if I can somehow win Lucian's heart and convince him it's time to try to love again… if I can be the one that, through love, can finally give him a dragonling that can save the world… how can I say no to that? I can't. Even if it might kill me."

Rachel was just shaking her head. Cinaed's lips were pressed tight, as if he'd run out of things to say.

Arabella's gaze was drawn out the window to the soaring mountains painted silver by the moonlight. She drifted to the glass and pressed her hands to it. This was Lucian's world—filled with magic, perched in a castle of glass on the top of a mountain. Who was she to think she could ever fit in here? Much less that she was the one to fulfill some kind of world-shaking treaty? It seemed like madness.

A small glint caught her eye in the distance. Something was moving out there—*flying*—and when she watched for it again, she caught the golden flash of a golden wing soaring through the night and headed for the keep.

"Cinaed," she whispered, gesturing him over with a wave of her hand.

He joined her at the window. "That's him, my

lady." He looked to her, waiting to see what she would say.

She looked down. She wasn't dressed for some kind of big confrontation—she was still in her bikini and a white t-shirt she had thrown over it as a cover up. All of it was soaking wet. But none of that mattered.

"I need to talk to him, one way or the other," she said to Cinaed. "Because it's stupid and childish to just ignore what's happening with what's at stake here."

Cinaed slowly nodded and said, "Go to him, my lady." He dropped his gaze to her body then bounced it right back up again to her eyes. "Just as you are. He won't be able to resist you."

She flushed with heat, and it seemed like cheating, showing up half naked at Lucian's door. But she didn't care—she would do whatever it took to get him to listen. She turned, and her bare feet made wet smacking sounds as she skittered across the stone floor of the pool room.

If she hurried, she would get to Lucian's lair before him.

Chapter Seven

LUCIAN LANDED WITH A THUD ON THE ROOF OF HIS lair.

He didn't sweep the keep for Arabella—he didn't need the confusing temptation of her scent right now. The flight back from Seattle had been spent in torment enough. His dragon wanted her, and soon enough, his wyvern form would, too. The only way to keep the realms apart was to mate with her... but that was much more likely to result in her death than to give him a dragonling. Not that his wyvern would care. With Cara, Lucian believed that if only his love were strong enough, it would carry them through. But it hadn't been. And it didn't.

And he'd already pushed Arabella away far too

much. He'd hurt her in an attempt to save her. If they mated, those doubts would come back to haunt him… and it would only result in her death, and his shortly afterward. Because there was zero possibility of him enduring that again—he was on the edge of turning wyvern as it was. No matter what path he took, there were none that ended with him fulfilling the treaty and several that ended with Arabella's death.

He much preferred to die first.

And he was running out of time for that option, too.

As his boots stomped heavily down the spiral staircase to his lair, he contemplated just how much time he actually had. The appearance of his wyvern had shaken him to the core. There was no way to know for certain if he had hours or days or weeks. The only safe course was to fly away to his dying place. *His tomb.* Like every dragon nearing the end of his life, he had prepared one. He didn't relish inhabiting it, and certainly not so soon.

But he might not have a choice if he wanted to keep her safe.

Lucian hesitated in the hallway outside his bedroom. He should consult with his brothers, make plans—because abandoning all hope of securing the treaty had far more ramifications beyond just his pathetic life, and soon, his death. He could at least help pave the way with them for the coming times of trouble, even if he wouldn't be there to join the fight. But the hour was past midnight, and truth be told, he was still exhausted —the world had taken its toll on him. He could do with more rest before facing his fate. In the morning, he would have the energy for his final preparations. He waved open the door to his bedroom and strode in.

He only got three steps before he stumbled to a stop.

Arabella stood in the middle of his room, barely clothed, skin still damp, her white t-shirt clinging wetly to her delicate body, showing every curve, her wet hair draped in long lumps down her chest.

He blinked. For an insane moment, he thought he was having some kind of dream.

"I let myself in." Her words were hesitant. Her hands trembled a little as she held them palm up when she shrugged. "You haven't changed the passcode."

He rubbed a hand over his eyes, but she was still there. "Why…" His tongue was thick, but now that his mind was grasping the fact that she was truly here—*truly standing half naked in his bedroom*—her scent washed over him in a wave that nearly dragged him under. He reeled from it, unable to form words.

"Lucian, please. Just hear me out." The look on her face made it clear—she thought he might throw her out. In reality, he was having to root his boots to the floor to keep from throwing her into his bed and having his way with her. One last time. One last taste of life…

"Arabella." No more words would come.

"Please." She edged toward him. "I know everything." She took two more steps, now only a half dozen feet away. Her nipples were taut under some barely-there swimsuit that was making his mouth ache.

Her words registered in his mind. "What do you know?" he asked, frowning.

"I know that your wyvern form is threatening to come out, and that means you're close to the end." A step closer, then another. "I know you're running out of time to fulfill the treaty, and that not fulfilling the treaty threatens everyone, human and dragons alike." Another step. *Holy mother of magic,* he could reach right out and touch her now. She dropped her voice. "I know you've been to the city to hook up with women. That you're searching for a new mate again. And I just have one question."

"A question?" he asked, his mind befuddled and intoxicated by her nearness.

"Did you find someone else? Someone who could love you more than I do?" She blinked fast like she was holding back tears.

He just stared at her in wonder.

"Because if you have," she said, "then I'll walk away. I'll step aside and let her love you and try to give you a dragonling. But if you haven't… if there's any chance…" Tears glistened at the corners of her eyes.

He couldn't breathe. His heart was threatening to stop in his chest as well.

She visibly swallowed. "If there's any way you'll let me, I want to love you, Lucian Smoke. I *already* love you. And I can't swear that it's a True Love, not the kind that will fulfill the treaty, because *dammit* I don't even know what love is, except… I know that I *do* love you… and I can't stand the thought of you hurt or dying or turning into some kind of wild animal or… or… in the arms of someone else…" The tear grew fat and full at the corner of her eye, and it held him hostage right up until it dropped… and then it unlocked something inside him.

"Stop." His words were hoarse, a gasp of pain. He seized her by the shoulders to silence the words that were slicing him to ribbons. He pulled her close, and she just blinked up at him with glassy eyes. "It was always you, Arabella. It will always *be* you."

She gasped, then sobbed, then the barest bit of a smile tugged at her lips.

"I need you," he whispered, pulling her even closer, leaning in but not kissing her, not yet. "So badly. Please be with me."

Her tears were flowing, but her smile shone through them. "Always."

And then he didn't care anymore, and he couldn't stop himself if he did.

He crashed his lips down on her, devouring and demanding, tasting her and breathing her in. He brushed back her wet hair, and held her head with both hands, consumed by the act of kissing her. All the darkness in his soul was banished by that simple act, the mere fact of touching her, holding her, connecting his soul with hers once again. Her hands clawed at his shoulders, and her body was climbing him, trying to get closer. Even with her barely-there swimsuit, there were too many clothes between them. He needed every inch of her body in his possession, the soft canvas of her skin laid bare for his touch.

With a flick of his hand, he magicked away his own clothes. She gasped, and her hands were a soft torture on his bare skin, but he broke their kiss long enough to seize her wet shirt and pull it free of her body. He didn't want to risk shifting with her in the room, so the rest had to come off the conventional way, but he made quick work of sliding off her bottoms and releasing the top with its ties. Her naked and chilled body was goosebumped all over, her breasts standing at perky attention in a way that made his mouth water.

He lifted her in one quick motion, wrapping her legs around his back as he quickly walked her to his bed. The feel of her bare arms around him, her pointed nipples brushing his chest, the heat of her sex so near his cock... he needed to be inside her. *Now.*

There would be time for slowness and softness later. He would spend his last night making love to her, not sleeping... and suddenly the rightness of that was so profound it was like the heavens had opened and a choir of angels had blessed his bed.

He laid her down in it, not disconnecting with her for even a moment, which left her legs wrapped around his back and her hands buried in his hair, pulling him in for more kissing. More sweetness and heat, the salt of her tears mixing with the heady scent of her sex. She was everything good and right in the world, the essence of humanity that he and every dragon loved and cherished and protected— and he would have her for one more night before the final release of death set him free of the world and its torturous, impossible demands.

He lifted from devouring her mouth to taste the glory of her neck. "My sweet, sweet Arabella," he said between kisses. "I need you *now,* my love."

"I am yours," she breathed, and there was such submission in it, such a giving over and pledging of her heart that it nearly brought tears to Lucian's eyes. He wasn't deserving of the great gift of her love, but he snatched it up and breathed it in, greedy for it. Because he *needed* it more than anything in any realm. More than he needed her body, which was well-nigh an impossible thing for him to deny at the moment.

He pulled her hands free from his hair, laced his fingers with them, and held them over her head, pressed deep into the comforter of his bed. His cock was aching, pressed against the heat of her skin and so near her sex, but not where he needed it. She bucked her hips against him.

He squeezed her hands, both trapped in his and planted above her head, in response. "Lie still, sweet one. So I can make you mine." He could barely breathe, his need was so great, but she stopped grinding against him long enough for him to pull back, angle just right, and thrust his cock deep inside the hot sweetness of her body.

His groan was loud and nearly covered the shriek that pried loose from her.

But staying still wasn't an option. He pulled back and thrust deep again, eliciting another shriek, this one heavily laced with a moan. She was so damn tight, it felt like he was taking her anew with each stroke. His breath was ragged with need as he thrust inside her again and again. He could feel her quiver around him, and her whimpers and struggles against the hold he had on her, keeping her hands pinned and her body subject to his pounding, told him she was rushing already toward release. He shifted his angle, diving deeper and pulling a moan so visceral from her that it had him quickening toward his own release as well.

"Holy fuck… Arabella…" He was panting as he

took her, words strangling in his mouth. He wanted
—nay, *needed*—her to reach her peak because he
simply couldn't last. She was too hot, too tight, too
beautiful in her open-mouthed gasps of pleasure.

"Oh God, Lucian… Oh God…" Her voice
pitched up, and then she was bucking and shrieking
underneath him, crying out his name and her love
and pulsing all around his cock in a symphony of
ecstasy that he had no power to resist. He roared
through his own release. Shooting hot pleasure
gushed from him and into her, emptying him of
everything that he was… every hope and dream he
had belonged to her. It went on and on, and when it
was finally spent, he released her hands and
collapsed by her side, just barely keeping his weight
off her as his entire body went limp. It pulsed with
waves of after-pleasure, and he quickly needed
more of her touch. He gathered her close against
him, her back to his chest, her breasts in his hands,
his face in her hair.

"Arabella, my love, you are my treasure, my
treasure, all mine, forever mine." He was babbling.
Delirious in her scent and the pleasure of her body.

She said nothing, just wrapped her arms around
his, holding him.

His hands gloried in the fullness and weight of

her breasts, but when her nipples teased quickly to life again under his attention, he knew he could give her even more pleasure than that quick, possessive taking he couldn't resist. His body still needed a moment or two to resurrect, but he could easily give her an orgasm, or three, before he was ready to go again.

He kept one hand kneading the delicious softness of her breast while the other drifted down to her sex. Her sharp intake of breath was all the validation he needed that she was ready for more.

"Lucian, you don't have to…"

He smiled the widest smile that had ever graced his face. Too bad she couldn't see it with his nose buried deep in her hair.

"Oh, yes I do, my love," he whispered with a laugh in his voice. "Again and again. Just try to stop me."

But her legs parted to give his hand better access, and he knew that *stopping* wasn't on either of their minds. Not tonight.

Her whimper as he stroked the slick heat of her sex was the most beautiful sound he'd ever heard. And he would have his way with her repeatedly tonight. He would indulge in her—in loving and possessing and pleasuring—until the dawn broke.

And when she was sated beyond measure, when she was so weary from his lovemaking that she simply couldn't take any more and drifted into a deep and satisfied sleep… then, and only then, would he be able to wrench himself away.

But he banished all thoughts of leaving as she moaned and bucked back against him.

For now—in this time and this space—there was only Arabella.

And his love for her.

Chapter Eight

Arabella awoke to the feel of Lucian entering her from behind.

She pulled in a breath, rising from the deep, dreamless sleep she'd fallen into. *What a glorious way to wake up,* was the only thought in her head. He was spooned behind her, cuddling her. His thick, long cock eased into her, stretching and filling her as if that were the most natural thing in the world. As if he belonged inside her, just as she belonged by his side, in his arms. When he'd filled her completely, he eased out again, a slow, seductive lovemaking that was as natural as breathing… only her breathing was decidedly unnatural, hitching a little as he left her body and then slowly pressed in again.

"Are you awake, my love?" he asked, whispering teasingly in her ear. He had to know, given the way her body was reflexively arching to give him better access. Damn, he felt good. She'd already lost count of how many times they'd coupled, and even more, how many times he'd brought her to climax. It was just like that first night, an endless haze of love-making and ecstasy. The room was still dark around them, so they hadn't literally fucked until dawn.

Yet.

He bottomed out inside her, then slowly started to withdraw again. "God, Lucian," she said, squirming against him and reaching behind her to keep him inside. "What you do to my body…" But her efforts were futile—he was slow and relentless in his pace, completely in control, and if she was honest, she loved that teasing part of him. The lightness and love of it. And she sure as hell couldn't argue with the result—the orgasms just got more mind-blowing with each new peak.

"Do you like what I do to your body?" he asked, the teasing even more arched.

Oh, God, what was he planning now? She was getting to know his rhythms in bed. He was a tremendously gracious lover, not to mention hot as hell. But he had his moments when he liked to draw it out, make her suffer in her need for release, make her beg while she was on the edge of that precipice, hanging and hanging and hanging… until he finally made her come.

And then it knocked her straight out.

She figured that was why he did it—to pleasure her more—but it could be that he simply enjoyed the torment. He got off on getting her off. It made her smile, and her heart swell, all at once. It was so like him… this brave, bold, strong man she was hopelessly in love with.

Lucian plunged deep inside her, then rolled her on the bed so that she was face down on the mattress. The pillows and sheets were long gone, tossed over the side by the turbulence of their lovemaking.

"You're not answering me, my love." There was wickedness in his voice. Then he pulled out only to plunge deep inside, still taking her from behind but now at a new angle with her legs held together and him driving straight down into her.

"Holy fuck!" she gasped as he hit a spot inside her that squealed its delight.

He chuckled lightly. "I'll take that as a *yes*. And a *more please.*"

"More… please…" she panted. He had her pinned, but it wasn't like she was complaining. Quite the opposite. And then he abandoned that leisurely pace and started pounding, long and deep, banging that spot again and again. She flat-out shrieked and cried for more. His hands found her hair and held her head down, not that she was in any danger of going anywhere. Her arms were sprawled to the side. Her legs were held tight together by his on either side. She was completely at the mercy of his unrelenting dominance of her body, pile-driving into her hard and fast and deep. She floated on the complete submission of it, the knowledge that he would take her as far as she could go and push her over the edge into bliss… and when the orgasm came, it rocked her, body and soul. She heaved off the bed, screaming and clenching the mattress in her hands, white-hot pleasure ripping through her in wave after wave after wave.

When he growled his release and stayed buried deep inside her, covering her body with his, fully and completely, it was the closest and most bare she had ever felt with him. She had given herself over to him, and he had wrenched out unbelievable pleasure for them both.

It took long minutes for their breathing to calm. For their bodies to settle. But he stayed buried in her, whispering sweet things into her ear, nuzzling her face and her hair and her neck.

God, she couldn't possibly love this man any more than she did. Like, it literally wasn't possible to feel more love than this without dying of it. If this wasn't True Love, she didn't think such a thing was even possible. Because *this* was everything. *He* was everything. Her entire universe wrapped up in a hot, manly body that was melded in pure bliss with hers.

Eventually, and with a long, low groan, he left her body and rolled next to her on the bed.

"Holy mother of magic," he breathed.

She grinned and lifted up on her elbows to see him. He was sprawled on his back, arms loose at his sides, the picture of complete satiation.

"Did you like that, my love?" she asked, the grin about ready to break her face.

He pulled a breath and blew it out like a sigh. "No man has ever loved a woman more thoroughly than I loved you just now, Arabella Sharp."

The happiness threatened to make her heart burst. "Well, we might as well stop now, then. We'll never top that."

He picked his head up and looked her like she was insane. "Bite your tongue, woman."

She licked her lips instead.

He groaned. "Never mind, that's my job." Then he leaned over and kissed her thoroughly, nipping at her tongue and her lips along the way. Then he moved his small love bites to her chin and then her neck, then her shoulder, and damn... if that wasn't sending a thrill straight to her core again. Everything this man did turned her on.

As he nibbled his way across her shoulders, a rough hand alternately gripping her bottom and caressing it, she wondered if this would be the night. Would he seal her right away? Would they start trying to make a dragonling right here in the dark of night in his bed? It occurred to her that she had no idea what that even entailed.

"My love?" she asked, twitching a little as his kisses tickled her back.

"Mm, hmm." It wasn't really an answer. He was busy exploring her body with his tongue.

She almost didn't ask... but she needed to know. If it was tonight, she needed to prepare, at least mentally. "What is involved in the sealing?"

Her words were quiet, but he froze mid-kiss. Then he hovered there, lips close to her back, his breath still hot on her skin, a long moment before answering. And when he did, the answer was in the form of his tongue painting a long, hot, wet line up her back, until he reached her shoulder. Then he kissed it and leaned back to look in her face.

"It's not unlike what we just did." His hand squeezed her bottom then drifted up her back, following that wet line.

"There's lovemaking involved?" She lifted her eyebrows. "This is even better than I thought."

He brushed the hair back from her face and caressed her cheek with his thumb. He stayed quiet so long, just gazing into her eyes, searching them for what, she had no idea… she didn't think he was going to say any more.

Finally, he ran his hand down her back again. "Yes, lovemaking. And much more than that. Although the lovemaking is the best you'll ever experience, so there's that." He was suddenly quiet, reserved, even as his fingers danced a light trail along her skin.

"Well, I guess we *can* top tonight, then." She peered at him, but he wasn't meeting her gaze.

He leaned forward and kissed her shoulder, then he lingered there, his naked body cuddled against her as his hand traced some intricate pattern on her back. "The sealing begins with lovemaking," he whispered. Quiet. Reverent. "The first time is just… ceremonial. An affirmation of the love between them. Some say it's essential for the female to be prepared. To open her heart to receive the magic. It may just be that the sealing is easier to endure when you're riding in the afterglow. Cara said it—" He stopped, both his words and the slow tracing on her back.

She twisted to look at him, but he was still avoiding her gaze.

He leaned forward to brush his cheek against her shoulder. Then he kissed it again. And then another. Then he was tracing a line of kisses across her back, between her shoulder blades, climbing up on top of her again, in the same position he had just used to make love to her. He swept her hair clear of her back.

"It starts here." He tapped a spot on her back, dead center between her shoulder blades.

She couldn't see what he was doing, so she didn't even try. Besides, her heart was hammering in her chest. He hadn't mentioned her—Cara, his previous mate—since that one time when Arabella feared he might jump off a cliff because of it. Her heart was telling her this conversation was just as dangerous.

"What starts there?" she asked, not looking back at him.

"The dragonfire seal." He leaned forward and kissed her back in the spot he just tapped. "I breathe a special fire, a mating fire, and it sears a magical rune into your skin." He was saying the words between kisses as he worked his way down her back. "It marks you as mine. It seals your body against the travails of carrying my dragonling. It changes you deep inside. The magic touches every cell of your body. Makes you as immortal as any dragon." His final kiss landed at the small of her back, just above her bottom. He pulled back, sitting lightly on her legs and caressing her curves with both hands. "Cara said the pain wasn't bad. But she always said things like that. Always said what I wanted to hear. What my heart needed."

Arabella held absolutely still. It felt like a magic spell had settled on them, loosening his tongue, getting him to speak about this. She didn't want to shatter it.

When she spoke, it was quiet, barely above a whisper. "What happens next?"

He kept caressing her bottom. "The dragonfire leaves a rune on your body. This is true for all dragons, but because I have fae blood, the runes are even more powerful in protecting you. They enliven my runes, and together, that brings all the magic to bear during the lovemaking that follows. That is when the dragonling is formed, crafted literally from the love and magic of its parents, formed in a womb that's bathed in ancient, immortal power." He leaned forward, sliding a hand up her back and hovering over her. He brushed her cheek with his lips, then whispered in her ear. "That time, when the dragonling is formed, the pleasure is indescribable. The sealing is finished with that, and then every time afterward, you're connecting with the same magic again. Mated lovemaking is ecstasy in a class all its own."

She could feel his erection pressing into her back, and she was likewise heating up with his words. He was leaving unspoken the things they both knew—that it was dangerous. That the dragonling might not survive. That *she* might not survive. But her love for him was already so intense. She couldn't imagine how mind-blowingly lost in him she would be *after* the sealing. Carrying his child. Helping him fulfill his duty and his destiny.

She wanted to say something, but words were clogging up in her throat.

Then he grabbed hold of her hair and pressed her forward, face down in the mattress again. He slid his hand down to hold her back, right at the point where the sealing would start, and his cock plunged into her, sudden and insistent. She gasped at the fullness of it. Always, every single time, it was like the first time with him. He was taking her hard and silent, plunging deep and holding her tight to keep her still. The pressure of her orgasm was growing fast, but the closeness with him was gone. He was distant—inside her but far from her—and she worried that she had pushed him too far, too fast. She opened her body to him, pushing back against his pounding, letting the sounds of her plea-sure escape her mouth as he drove himself harder and faster into her.

He would finish this lovemaking with a mind-blowing orgasm, just like all the rest. And, knowing Lucian, he would wake her five more times between now and dawn for more rounds of pleasure. But she wouldn't ask him any more tonight about the sealing.

It was still a raw wound for him, and she had to be careful about how to open it.

But they would have time for all of that later.

Then her mind was taken over by the screaming orgasm that was rippling through her, and all thoughts fled into white-hot pleasure and the darkness of night.

Chapter Nine

IT'S BETTER THIS WAY.

No matter how many times Lucian repeated that during his hour-long flight north, there was no *better* in how he felt. Then again, he was winging his way to his death, so that was to be expected.

The chilly Canadian Jetstream blew past his wings, chilling him to the bone, but he could still feel the slip of Arabella's silky hair through his human fingers, the soft warmth of her forehead as he kissed her one last time. He'd left her sound asleep, dropped into the depths of relaxation by their sexual adventures throughout the night. It was the perfect way to leave if leaving had to be done.

Which it did.

His brothers would have to manage the fallout

from his death without him. He hated every part of that—the fact that he was leaving them to deal with the unraveling of the treaty; that he would never have a true chance to say goodbye to Arabella; and not least, his own death—but it was the only way to save her. The world might go to hell, but the woman he loved wouldn't have to die trying to save it.

It's better this way.

He almost believed it now.

Lucian dipped down from the slipstream and dove into a rocky canyon that wove deep into the Canadian Rockies. Every responsible dragon sought out a final resting place well ahead of his five-hundredth birthday. Some desperately tried to stall the inevitable by impregnating any female they could seduce—or took by force, in the case of the House of Drakkon. And several other of the Houses, if he were honest about it. Lucian's position as the crown prince was an inherent part of protecting humanity from the fae, but policing his own kind had been a full-time occupation as well. Many were repulsed by the number of females who died in the mating process, yet most dragons managed to produce a dragonling at some point. But even when that bought them an additional five hundred years, they all succumbed to the wyvern in the end. If a dragon had successfully mated, their wyvern would *only* be a savage force of destruction, blasting dragonfire at will and hunting whatever it wished for meat. If the dragon *hadn't* mated before devolving into his wyvern form, it was even worse. The hunt would be for females as mates as well as prey.

An uncontrolled wyvern was not only hunted down and killed by its House for the sake of decency; the House itself risked war with other Houses, or the House of Smoke if no one else stepped up. A House that wouldn't slay their own wyvern was a House that had proved themselves a danger to all dragons.

Most would rather die in solitude than force their own House to tarnish their talons with their blood. For that, a pre-selected tomb was the preferred way to die—a secretive spot where a dragon could spend his final days contemplating his life and dying with honor. Some took a specially-prepared magical poison. Some willed their wyvern to come and beat itself bloody in an attempt to escape. The best among them used slow starvation as a way to atone for past sins and cleanse their minds in preparation for oblivion. Or perhaps prayed that the heaven the angels spoke of really existed and had room for dragons.

Lucian preferred starvation in concept, but he might not have the luxury of the time that would take.

His tomb was far enough from the keep to be not easily discoverable, but by custom, the dragons of one's family knew the location. And it was, by design, close enough to be easily accessible from the keep, in case his wyvern came on unexpectedly, and he needed to make haste in locking himself away. His beast was more dangerous than most, given the enhancements to his magic due to his fae blood, and it could wreak even more destruction on the human world.

And one human in particular.

Arabella.

His body still hummed from their lovemaking, and even the thought of her name brought a flush of pleasure that enervated the runes that danced along his skin. Their night of ecstasy had sealed his fate—after that, his dragon would never accept another as a mate. And his wyvern would seek her out preferentially, crossing mountains and countries to find her, passing up a hundred other women in his rampage to procreate.

No demon conjured from hell could force Lucian to allow that happen.

When he finally reached the spot he had chosen for his tomb, it was clear he hadn't been there for several decades. Not since that dark time after Cara died. In the years since, brambles had overgrown and half-blocked the entrance. The cave was tucked in the face of a sheer granite cliff, formed when a portion of the mountain had been pried away by weather, a trickling stream, and the passage of time. Lucian cleared the weeds out with a roaring blast of dragonfire as he landed, leaving him standing on the edge of the cliff amidst the charred remains, still smoking under his boots. He left them burning and set about placing the wards on his final resting spot.

He summoned his runes, which gathered into his hands until they turned almost black with the writhing lines. He slowly and methodically passed his hands over every inch of the rocky cavern, infusing the granite with spells that would keep dragons, fae, and any other magical creatures from invading his death chamber. He spoke the incantations, a mixture of fae and dragontongue, in a slow chant that settled his mind and body as each spell locked into place, interwoven with the others, a complex net of ritual, deep magic that would be impenetrable to all… including himself. His brothers might come for him, but they wouldn't be able to pass this magical barrier. Lucian alone held the key to unlocking it, and once he turned wyvern, even that would be lost along with his rational mind. There would be no turning back at that point —his wyvern would rail against the magic, breathe dragonfire and rip the rock with its claws, but it would die of starvation before it could dig its way out.

Many a dragon had been entombed over the millennia this way, forever sealed into a chamber of their choosing.

If Lucian were lucky, that's how it would come to pass for him as well. If he weren't, his brothers would find him and entreat him to change his mind.

He would try to be dead before that happened.

The cave wasn't large—just a nook in the mountain that narrowed to a crevice at the back— but it had enough space to pace its twenty-foot by twenty-foot length and stand up straight in the middle. The open face of it let in the cool mountain air, as well as the light from the sun rising over the back of the mountain behind him. The flat floor of granite wasn't comfortable, but it was level enough to sit. The wards would keep out anything magical, but there was no physical door that would keep anything from straying in. The open face would allow the crows to pick his bones clean.

Lucian passed his hands over that opening, speaking the last of the deep magic to ensure it was sealed, then he stepped back to survey his work. The place hummed with magical energy, a vibration that was soothing in its own morbid way. With the wards set and locked in place, he settled into the center of the cave, sitting with legs crossed and hands resting on his knees.

He spent a few minutes calming the pounding of his heart and contemplating his fate. It was cold —damn cold. Maybe hypothermia would take him before starvation. Although he judged that unlikely —the dragonfire in his blood was enough to fire a small village. His human form was more vulnerable to the cold, but he was unlikely to freeze to death. Just as he was urgently regretting his lack of an adequate poison, a strange buzzing started in his pants. It took him a moment to realize it was his phone.

He stood, fished it out of his pocket, and stared at the face.

Leksander.

Lucian let it go to message.

He gazed out of the cave at the orange-pink clouds set afire by the rising sun. His House was waking. It was only a matter of time before Leksander realized Lucian wasn't at the keep. It wouldn't be long after before he tracked him here.

Lucian crushed the phone in his fist until he was sure the GPS was ruined, then he got up and threw it out of the cave and watched the glittering pieces fall into the gloomy pre-dawn murk.

He was running out of time to die.

There was one way to make sure his brothers couldn't talk him out of this path he'd chosen—by turning wyvern before they could reach him. There was no reasoning with his beast, and no coming back from it, once he fully turned.

And quiet contemplation wasn't the way to make that happen.

Lucian stepped back from the edge and sat in the middle of his self-selected tomb. Then he envisioned the one great sin he had committed, the one he'd been paying penance for ever since. *Cara.* All the images he'd tried to forget over the years. All the sounds. The feel of her blood. The tearing of her flesh under his own talons. The wet dripping blood of his unborn child being ripped from her womb.

The screams he would never forget. The utter silence of the tiny dragon baby who refused to breathe. The complete certainty that he was responsible for all of it—their pain, their suffering, their deaths.

He let his mind go there, reliving the horror and the grief in an endless loop of agony.

A roar sounded in his ears, and searing dragonfire billowed around him. His screams echoed off the walls, his own dragonfire curled back on him, searing him, burning a penance into him that would never be enough.

He sat and waited for the wyvern to come.

Chapter Ten

WHEN ARABELLA AWOKE, SHE FELT SO GOOD, SHE thought she might still be dreaming.

She stretched her body wide across the sheets, expecting to bump her arm or elbow or leg against Lucian's naked form, but she didn't. Her eyes popped open, and a quick glance around the bedroom showed he was missing.

"Lucian?" she called, in case he was just in the bathroom—although, with the size of Lucian's bedroom, that was twenty-five feet away. He might not even hear her. She groaned and flopped her head back on the mattress. The sun was streaming through the windows, and she felt like she had finally slept hard *forever.* Lucian had given her body an Olympic-sized workout throughout the night, and she was aching—deliciously—all over. She closed her eyes again and stretched the aches and pains out a little more before rolling up to sitting and resolving to actually go hunt for the man.

She checked the bathroom first, but it was empty. She called his name again, but no answer. It wasn't until she padded down to the kitchen, and there was still no sign of him, that she started to get concerned.

There was no reason for him to leave the lair.

She looked down and realized she was still naked from their night's activities, and if she was going to go prowling around the keep after him, it was probably best she got dressed. She jogged back up the steps, her body still filled with a low-humming buzz from the endless orgasms. It was giving her energy now that she was awake. She reached his bedroom and realized that all she had was a bikini and the still damp t-shirt from the night before. Lucian had always conjured clothes for her, which presented a slight problem.

She frowned. It was unlike him to be so thoughtless, taking off without at least leaving her something to wear. She dug through his wall-to-wall closet, looking for something that wouldn't be ridiculously oversized.

Her heart started to kick up a beat, and panic nibbled at the edge of her mind.

He had left her naked in bed.

There was no note, no sign of him.

He'd left without a thought to her and what she would find upon waking.

By the time she happened upon a slim black dress at the back of his closet, her mind was in a full-blown panic.

Something had happened, something bad, something that he had to leave immediately for and couldn't take the time even to leave her a note. She snatched the dress off the hanger and slipped it over her head before realizing it was some kind of cocktail dress, all shimmery and satin with tiny black pearls stitched into the neckline.

She froze. Why would Lucian have a cocktail dress in his closet?

She didn't need anyone to point out the obvious to her—*this was Cara's.* His previous mate. He'd held onto it for some reason, some sentimental reason, and here Arabella was throwing it on her body— the one he had so recently fucked and then abandoned.

She couldn't get the dress off fast enough.

With tears in her eyes, she scrambled back over

the disarray of the bedroom, searching for her bikini and t-shirt. She had barely gotten them on when she heard someone calling her name downstairs. Rushing barefoot to the door of the bedroom and down the spiral staircase, her heart was trying to outrace her mind in how fast it could imagine what horrible thing had happened.

"There you are!" It was Rachel, standing in Lucian's kitchen with Cinaed.

"What are you guys doing here?" Arabella asked, but her heart was in her throat. Something was wrong. Something was terribly, terribly wrong.

"He's gone, my lady." Cinaed's face held such worry that Arabella's anxiety just zoomed through the roof.

Her chest squeezed like a mountain was crashing down on her. "Gone *where?*"

"We thought you might know," Rachel said. She and Cinaed exchanged a look, then they turned back to her. "How did it go last night?"

Oh no. "Fine. Great." But the way her voice hiked up belied the truth. It *had* gone well… right up until the moment she pressed him too hard, wanting to know about the sealing. Forcing him to remember what he had gone through with Cara. *Oh God…* she had driven him off.

Rachel was looking her up and down with a scowl. "Well, you've got your walk of shame clothes on. Normally I would take that as a good sign. But you don't sound so good, sister. What happened?"

Cinaed was also giving her a questioning look.

"I… we…" *Oh God*, she was already fucking up. It didn't matter how much sex they'd had, she'd said the wrong thing and broke his heart. Or just stabbed ugly memories into it. She knew how close he was to the edge with all of that. How could she possibly explain to Cinaed and Rachel what had happened?

"You need not tell us every detail," Cinaed said, but there was a stridency in his voice. "We just need to know if you have any idea where he's gone."

She shook her head. "He left me…" She swallowed, a flush of heat coming to her face. "He was gone when I woke up."

Rachel squeezed her eyes shut and shook her head. When she opened them, her eyes had an ocean of sympathy. Cinaed was rubbing his face and appeared to be thinking furiously.

"He's not in the keep," he said. "And he's not answering his phone. Leksander thinks…" He looked up from his stern study of the floor in front of him and met Arabella's gaze. "Leksander thinks he's gone to the tomb."

"The what?" Arabella asked. She looked to Rachel, but she just shrugged. "You mean, like the tomb of his dead… *mate?*"

Cinaed blinked and leaned back. "No, of course not. That's in… well, that's far away. He wouldn't go back there, in any event, no matter how, well… *upset* he was." He peered at her. "Was he upset?"

"Not exactly." Arabella grimaced. "Maybe. I might've said something that maybe upset him?" *Oh God, this was all her fault.*

Cinaed nodded. "It is hard to tell with my prince. His heart is locked away. I thought, perhaps, with you…" He shook his head. "It doesn't matter. But tell me this—did his wyvern come out? Is that what made him flee?"

"No." About that, she was sure. "He was completely in control the whole time. There was no hint of any of that. We were making plans… I mean, I thought we were making plans…" Her shoulders dropped. "I have no idea what was actually going through his head." All she could think about was how he had shut down… and now he was gone. There was no way those two things were unrelated. She was definitely to blame for whatever had happened. And that just made her chest squeeze harder.

Cinaed swore in a language that sounded old and Irish. "If Leksander is right, and he's gone to the tomb—"

"*What* is this tomb you keep talking about?" Rachel interrupted him.

He gave her a soft look, and it occurred to Arabella that she had no idea what had transpired between the two of them. She'd left them alone in a pool room with just their swimsuits. They were raging pissed at each other at the time, and Arabella had been gone with Lucian all night. The two of them... well, nothing would surprise her, at this point. But she didn't have time to worry about any of that.

"The tomb is where dragons go to die." Cinaed's voice was heavy.

Oh God. "Cinaed."

"I know, my lady," he said. "We must go there at once. Only... I don't know where it is. That's something entrusted to family members." He grimaced and studied the floor again.

"Well, get this Leksander person to tell us," Rachel said, impatient.

"He's already left the keep. I think he's headed

there."

"What about Leonidas?" Arabella asked.

"He's on his way back from Seattle, but that will take time." Cinaed was pacing again, muttering to himself. "But this is a matter of life and death, and protocol be damned." Then he stopped and turned back to Arabella. "You must come with me to address the king and queen. For you, in this case, surely they would break with convention. And they must be out of their minds with worry, in any event, assuming…"

Arabella's heart was lurching around with every word. "Assuming *what?*"

He frowned. "Assuming they even know what's going on." He flicked a look at her bare feet and back up to her eyes. "Although, one look at you, my lady, and they'll be able to discern it well enough."

What did he mean by that? But she didn't really care. "Cinaed, you have to know I would do anything to make sure Lucian is all right." She looked down at her clothes. "But I can't go see the king and queen like this."

"Agreed," he said. "Perhaps you can borrow some of Leonidas's substantial female wardrobe."

Arabella arched her eyebrows but just nodded. "Let's go."

The three of them hurried out of Lucian's apartment and through the keep to Leonidas's. Cinaed explained quickly that he would hardly miss whatever she wished to take. Rachel ran through the closet of women's clothes like a hurricane, tossing things through the air and searching for something suitable for presenting to royalty. Cinaed insisted that it did not matter as long as she had actual clothing on, but Rachel shushed him with such fervor that he quickly gave up. It only took her a moment to pull together something long and white and flowing. It was practically a bridal dress, but Arabella didn't care. She tugged it on, and Cinaed barely had time to turn his back, before she was dressed and ready to go.

He led them on a long walk to the far side of the keep. Arabella was expecting a throne room or some kind of grand receiving hall, but instead, he brought her to a lair like all the rest, only this one had a clear crystal carving of a pair of dragons—their long tails curled down the side of the doorway, and their heads rested on each other's shoulders in a dragon-type embrace. One had sapphire blue jewels for eyes whereas the other had deep amber ones.

Cinaed rang the bell or did something at the

door that seemed to be the magical equivalent of knocking. After a moment, a gorgeous and refined older version of Lucian appeared at the door. Arabella had to do a double take before she realized that, of course, this wasn't Lucian, but rather his father, the king. He had that same timeless look, only as if he had worn it for a few more centuries. And he was dressed in the same sort of ancient hoodie-type clothing that Arabella had seen on Lucian when he first revealed his dragon nature.

"Your Highness." Cinaed bowed his head in an elaborate ritual greeting. "May I present Arabella Sharp and her maid, Rachel. We have a request of great urgency, sire."

"Of course, of course, come in, Cinaed." The king gave him a warm but sad smile." You are, naturally, here about my son."

"Yes, sire."

The king floated his gaze past Cinaed to give Arabella a gentle glance. "My dear, you are as lovely as I have imagined."

Arabella's throat was closing up, but she managed to clear it and say, "It's a pleasure to meet you."

He seemed to draw in a breath, then examine her more closely. "I see you do not as yet bear the seal of my son." He let the breath out like a long sigh, then he turned to Cinaed. "I fear it may be too late."

"I refuse to give up!" Cinaed said roughly, then pulled back, chastened. "I mean, we mustn't give up hope, your Highness."

The king's sad smile returned. "And now you sound like the queen. Which, I'll have you know, puts you in good stead. She is rarely wrong." Then he backed away from the door in slow steps that were at once regal and somehow ancient. If Arabella's count was correct, he had to be close to a thousand years old. She could hardly wrap her mind around it.

The three of them shuffled into the king's lair at his beckoning.

Inside, the queen was standing at the two-story windows that flooded their great room with light. Her back was to them, and at first, all Arabella could see was her incredibly gorgeous hair, chestnut brown and tumbling down her back to below her waist. She was wearing some kind of yellow sundress that flared and billowed out from her waist as if it were made of a hundred gossamer layers rippling gently in an unseen wind.

"We have company, my love." The king

gestured them forward.

The queen turned to face them, and her brilliant blue eyes, so much like Leonidas's, were bright with tears that had yet to fall. Her gaze immediately found Arabella. She frowned and looked to Cinaed. "So this is the one he chose?"

Arabella's heart seized, and she glanced at Rachel. To her best friend's credit, she was keeping her very sarcastic lips buttoned. But Arabella could tell she was on high alert and already taking a dislike to the queen—and at the ready to come to Arabella's defense, if necessary.

Which seemed crazy. This was Lucian's mother —she would love him as much or more as anyone. They had nothing but agreement about that.

"Yes, your Highness." Cinaed's voice was tense.

Arabella kept quiet, waiting for someone to give her a clue when it was her turn to speak.

The queen's gaze returned to her, and she slowly crossed the room with that same ancient yet elegant way of moving the king had. She kept examining Arabella as she approached, not speaking. Arabella felt like it was some kind of test, only she had no idea how to pass. As the queen got closer, Arabella could see Lucian's likeness in her— the same carved cheeks, the same proud bearing.

She took Arabella's hands and held them with her cool fingers.

Arabella tried to hide her shock.

The queen peered into her eyes. "He hasn't sealed you, yet, my dear."

Arabella shook her head, ashamed—was this the test? And did she just fail it?

The queen nodded. "He's afraid," she said, softly. Arabella heard a mother's heart breaking in that sad, regal voice. "He's hurting and afraid of losing you, just like Cara. And now he's fled."

Arabella nodded. Suddenly she wasn't anxious about anything the king or queen might think of her—all she wanted was to know Lucian was all right. "What can I do?"

The queen didn't quite smile, but she gave a nod that felt like one. "You might be the only thing that could bring him back."

"I've already sent Leksander, my love," the king said from behind them.

"And I already told you that wouldn't work." What must've been an epic fight between them seemed to be a mere disagreement, at least as much as they would show in front of others.

Arabella squeezed the queen's hands, bringing her attention back.

More of a smile appeared on the queen's face.

"I'll do anything I can," Arabella said.

"Give us leave to visit the tomb," Cinaed said. "I'll see her there, and I'll make sure he comes back to you, your Highness."

The queen bestowed an even warmer smile on him. "The treaty depends on him, Cinaed. I've been holding off my own visit to the tomb these many years in the perpetual hope that my son would finally find his way. I don't know if you'll succeed, Cinaed, but you're a good man for trying." She turned back to Arabella. "As for you, young one… I suspect you may be all that he lives for now. You may have more power in your heart than the rest of us combined. Go after him, please. I pray that your love is True and that you can bring him back. To all of us. The world needs him."

"*I* need him." The words were out before Arabella could think about how foolish they sounded.

But they brought a genuine smile the queen's face. "Then go. *Hurry.*"

Arabella barely had time to nod before Cinaed's hand was on her arm, tugging her toward the door of the king and queen's lair.

She didn't even have time to thank them.

Chapter Eleven

Lucian's inner torment was interrupted by an ancient curse.

"Thanos-sut," Leksander spat at him. "You're a fucking idiot." The first part was dragontongue, and it roughly meant *balls for brains,* and the second part was obvious. Both were probably true, but Lucian didn't care.

"Go away." He closed his eyes again, hoping against hope that Leksander would concede this fight before it even started. Lucian was still locked inside the wards placed around his tomb, so his brother couldn't force him to do anything. If he wanted to flap his lips from his spot at the edge of the cave, where he precariously perched in his human form, he was welcome to it. Or he could fly back the way he came. Lucian would simply ignore him and stay where he was, sitting on the hard granite floor, the cold just beginning to seep through his clothes.

"Not until you get off your ass and do your duty."

Lucian ignored him. But in spite of his best efforts to tune out his brother's words, they wormed their way into his head. What Lucian was doing would bring dishonor to his House—and a whole lot worse—but he wasn't going to risk Arabella's life just to say he *tried.* Ultimately, he would fail, and that was all that mattered in the end. He didn't need to take her down with him.

Leksander roared, and Lucian heard a whoosh of wings against air.

He waited two heartbeats, then another, but he couldn't help looking... only to see a blue fireball soaring toward him. It hit the wards, crackled and splintered and splashed all around, but didn't penetrate the protective magic he had set up.

Dammit. Leksander should have known that wouldn't work. Then again. Leksander's magic was stronger than his—Lucian had always known this, but Leksander's recent curing of the vampire brought that into bold relief.

Too bad his brothers couldn't fulfill the treaty for him. Both were better suited to it.

Lucian glared as Leksander winged his silver dragon closer to the cave. Lucian braced himself for another blast of dragonfire, praying the wards would hold as his mind raced—*what would he do if his brother breached the barrier?*—but Leksander just landed on the lip of the cave, nose up against the wards, his runes writhing across his now-human skin.

"What do I have to do to convince you to stop pouting like a child and come out and do your duty?" Leksander's ice-blue eyes were alive with anger. "Because I'm not letting you fuck this up, brother."

Lucian sighed. But Leksander had given up on magic, so that trickled relief through him. "It's no use, Leksander. My dragon has already bonded with her."

"So why are you here instead of sealing your mate?" His anger leaked small wisps of dragonfire from the corners of his mouth.

Lucian gritted his teeth. "You know why."

"She's not fated to be like Cara. That woman—"

Lucian was on his feet, flying at the ward barrier before he even blinked. *"Don't you even—"*

"Or what?" Leksander challenged. They were inches apart, just the pulsing magic of the wards between them. "You'll come out and dip your talons in my blood? Because I'd like to see you try, brother."

Anger seethed across Lucian's skin as his runes twitched to be used. Leksander was baiting him, but he couldn't help responding. He was a raw nerve, and his brother had just raked claws across it.

"There's only one way this ends," Lucian said through his teeth. "And I'll not have another woman's blood on my hands before I meet my fate."

"Your fate…" Leksander stopped, anger seeming to bind up his words. Then he pounded a fist on the barrier of the wards, which only sparked a flash of blue magic that threw his hand back. He roared— Lucian imagined the burn was intense—then he glared at Lucian once more. "Your fate is *not* to die in this cave. Not now. Not for hundreds of years, Lucian."

But it was. Then a thought—a strange and horrible thought—came into his head and electrified it like the magic lighting up his ward-protected prison.

"Do you really want to help me, my brother?" Lucian asked.

Leksander frowned and pulled back.

"Don't let me turn wyvern in this rocky grave," Lucian added quickly. "Put me out of my misery. End my torment."

Leksander snarled. *"Shut up* with that cowardice."

But a small smile snuck out on Lucian's face. Leksander looked at him like he had already lost his mind to his wyvern, but Lucian hurried on. "Not cowardice... *a loophole,* Leksander."

"What nonsense are you speaking?" But he looked uncertain.

"The treaty requires the *first surviving spawn* of the House of Smoke to carry on the line."

"I know it well enough—"

"So *kill me,* Leksander." His smile grew. "It may be five hundred years after my birth, but a death is still a death. Then the treaty would have to fall to Leonidas to fulfill. There no possibility the fae could argue otherwise. He *is* a spawn of the House of Smoke... and if he survives when I do not..."

Leksander's face twisted with disgust. "You know Leonidas cannot fulfill the treaty—"

"I know he cannot *fall in love.*" Lucian tipped his head—his brother had to know this part was true. "But Leonidas has raised *not falling in love* to an Art Form. He could do it, Leksander. He *will* do it—he *must;* you must see to it—after I pass. But kill me *now,* and swiftly. Who knows how much time any of us have before our wyverns arrive. Mine has already made an appearance."

"I will not kill you." Leksander seemed horrified that Lucian would even speak it.

"My brother… there's no hope for me." He softened his voice, pleading. He would beg if he had to. "I've already poisoned Arabella's mind with doubt. She would never survive the full term of carrying my dragonling. And her death would *end me…* for magic's sake, Leksander, I'm halfway to wyvern as it is!" Lucian edged as close to the wards as he could without feeling their wrath. *"Please,* my brother."

Torment twisted Leksander's face. His lips pressed tight, holding back something.

Just as Lucian prepared to flat-out beg his brother, Leksander spoke. "This is all to save Arabella."

"Yes, but—"

"Then I will kill her myself if nothing else will motivate you." He flung his arms wide.

"*What?*" Lucian cried.

But Leksander had already leaped backward off the edge of the cliff, shifting and catching the wind with his dragon's wings.

For a moment's breath, Lucian stared in horror as Leksander swooped up into the air and away from the mountain. Then a roar boiled up from deep inside Lucian's soul and erupted from his mouth. He shoved his hands forward, summoning all his runes in a rush to thrust aside the wards he had so carefully constructed. They were barely down before he leaped from the cave, shifting mid-air and pumping his wings to race after Leksander.

Stop! Lucian commanded, still a hundred yards from his brother.

But the mental demand reached him, and Leksander banked sharply left, coming back around toward him.

Take it back. Lucian was headed on a collision course for the silver dragon.

Make her your mate, Lucian. Leksander was winging straight for him.

You cannot force this on me. He was nearly there.

Blue magic crackled along Leksander's silver-colored scales. *The world needs you, Lucian—*

Fuck the world! He whipped his talons forward, dipping a wing to bank right and catch Leksander by the neck. He screamed, and dragonfire singed Lucian's tail, but they were grappled now… *and falling.* Spinning and flailing, a mass of wings and tails lashing, Lucian felt his brother's blood run over his talons, his blades digging deep into Leksander's neck and side. Lucian fought to catch the wind with his wings, and failing that, magic-boosted to slow their fall toward a rocky death a thousand feet below.

The slickness of Leksander's blood made Lucian lose his grip. Another cry, more dragon fire, and a slash of talons across Lucian's chest, but then Leksander was free of him, lofting himself up and backward to gain his freedom.

Lucian felt the hot spray of his brother's blood falling from above—Leksander's magic may be stronger, but Lucian was still a golden dragon. The most powerful dragon blood mixed with fae ancestry as well. It was possible that Leksander could grievously wound him in battle, but only if Lucian allowed it. Which he couldn't do as long as Arabella was in danger…

Don't make me kill you, Leksander, he begged. *Leave her alone.*

I had to knock some sense into you. His brother was slowly losing altitude.

It was then that Lucian could see the torn wing. Suddenly, his brother started dropping like a stone.

Goddammit, Leks. Lucian swooped down, catching up to his brother and ducking a golden wing under his tattered silver one. Together—two dragons, scale to scale, limping through the air— they managed to gain some altitude again and stay aloft long enough to land back at Lucian's tomb.

Lucian eased his brother against the rocky wall then stepped back.

Leksander shifted human, and the wounds were even more obvious. His arm was bent at an unnatural angle, and his body was smeared with blood, with a giant gash still ebbing blood.

"Thought you were going to kill me for a moment, there." Leksander's smile was painted with blood, and he slowly crumpled to the floor.

Lucian felt a black hole open inside him and swallow all feeling, all horror that he should rightly feel at this thing he had done. Leksander would survive—his wounds were horrible but not life-ending—but Lucian was clearly a danger to his brothers, not just Arabella.

"You threatened my mate." The words were simple and true, but they didn't fill the raging black hole inside him.

"*Make* her your mate, Lucian." Leksander's voice carried pain. "It's the only way."

Lucian blinked, fought against the blackness, then slowly shook his head. "No. There's another."

Then Lucian turned and took a running leap off the cave mouth ledge, hurtling himself into his dragon form before his brother could say something to stop him. Leksander couldn't follow, and Lucian knew in his heart that he wouldn't harm Arabella. Leksander had only been baiting him to get him out of the tomb.

But Lucian also knew his brother wouldn't give up. Leksander was a dragon hopelessly in love with an angeling—his brother was nothing if not relentless in the face of impossible odds.

What Lucian needed was someone not quite so sentimental about killing him.

The fae prince, Zephan, would do, but he was bound by the treaty to not harm members of the House of Smoke. And dragons were well-nigh impossible to kill by anything short of fae magic or the fate of their own wyvern. An angel blade would manage it, but good luck getting any of the angelings to listen, much less do as one wished—

Then a singular idea invaded his mind—a horrible one, but Lucian wasn't above stooping to any debasement to make this happen.

He turned north and flew further into Canada.

The only coven of vampires he knew in the area should be overjoyed to see him.

Lucian took solace from the fact that Leksander would be unable to follow him until he healed, and by then, it would be too late to witness his ignoble end at the hands—or rather fangs—of the bloodsuckers.

Chapter Twelve

RIDING A BLUE DRAGON WAS NOWHERE NEAR AS SEXY as flying a golden one.

The wind whipped Arabella's hair as she clung to Cinaed's back. His blue scales glistened like sapphire jewels—he was truly a beautiful dragon, even if his nearness didn't heat her up the way clinging to Lucian's golden scales did. But they were headed to see Lucian, so she was tense with antici- pation. The king and queen had given them the coordinates for his tomb, and Cinaed must have some kind of GPS in his head because he took off right away and was flying without any instrumenta- tion that she could see. But she could tell they were heading north, and it got colder and colder as they went.

They flew deep into the wilderness, leaving Seattle and the keep far behind. Eventually, right as her fingers turned so numb she was in danger of falling off, Cinaed swooped down into a canyon and weaved along it. Eventually, they came upon a small cave in the face of a granite wall. She might've missed the cave altogether, but there were burn marks all around the edges and the walls inside.

Her heart seized.

I'm sure he's fine, my lady. Cinaed's thoughts connected to hers, but they didn't reassure her.

When they got close enough to almost land, she saw a man inside the cave slumped against the rock wall, holding his arm and grimacing, eyes shut. For the two heartbeats that it took for them to touch down in the cave, Arabella was certain it was Lucian.

But her worst fears were beaten back in a flurry when the noise of their landing popped open the man's eyes, and she saw they were icy blue. And then, even in the murk, she could tell it wasn't Lucian at all—this had to be his brother, Leksander. There was a strong family resemblance, but it was clear that Leksander had inherited his mother's blue eyes, like Leonidas.

Arabella quickly scrambled off Cinaed's back,

and he shifted. She rubbed her arms and blew on her hands to warm them while she shuffled over to see Leksander. "Are you all right?" she asked as she knelt. He was covered in blood, but she knew that wasn't a good indicator of anything, not with dragons.

"Just taking a rest." Leksander used his hand to brace against the wall and boost up from the floor, but it was clear it was causing him pain.

Arabella rose with him. "You sure?"

He seemed to shake it off. "Quite." Then he peered at her. "Arabella Sharp, my brother is very much in love with you. And that almost cost me my hide."

Arabella frowned. What did that mean?

"The prince was already in his tomb," Cinaed guessed.

Leksander nodded. "I managed to bring him out, but…" He gazed off at the mountains below them. "He's run off again. I know not where."

"Shall I search for him?" Cinaed asked, quickly. "How long ago did he leave?"

"Not long, but he could be far by now." Leksander put his hand on Cinaed's shoulder. "I know you love him, my friend, but you don't possess the fae senses that I do. I need to be the one to look for him." He glanced at Arabella. "Lucian may yet return, and if he does, he'll want to see *you*. Remain here while I search, in case he comes back."

Without another word, Leksander slow jogged toward the edge of the cave and leaped into the air, shifting into a silver dragon as he went.

"So, we're just going to wait?" Arabella was looking all around the cave, thinking what a horrible place this would be to die. Not that there was a *good* place to die, but by yourself? In a lonely cave in the middle of nowhere?

"I'm sorry it's not more comfortable," Cinaed said, and he actually seemed to mean it.

"I'm not worried about that," she said, scowling. "I just can't believe…" She swallowed looking at the desolation of the cave again. "Why would he choose this, Cinaed? Is mating with me such an awful prospect that he would rather run away and die?" It was hard to keep the tremble out of her voice.

"No, my lady, *no.*" Cinaed took a step closer. He seemed like he wanted to give her a hug or something, but was holding himself back. "It's as the queen says—his heart was broken once, and I'm afraid that's not something he thinks he can endure again."

"But running away?" Arabella shook her head. "That doesn't sound like the man I know and love."

Cinaed frowned and dropped his gaze to the rough granite floor. "Pain of the heart does horrible things to a man." He looked up. "Especially a man who loves so deeply, as my prince does."

She had to agree with that. There was nothing *shallow* about Lucian Smoke.

A soft whisper of wings drew her gaze to the mouth of the cave. The silhouette of a dragon was winging through the sky toward them.

Arabella pointed. "Is Leksander coming back already?"

Cinaed's eyes shifted to dragon slits, something Arabella hadn't seen happen before. They quickly changed back to human. A small smile jumped onto his face. "No, my lady, it's the prince."

As the winged form drew closer, the sun glinted off his golden scales. Arabella's heart started pounding even as a gush of relief made her feel almost weak. The beauty and grace of him flying through the air gave way to a small glimmer of concern as he didn't seem to be slowing down.

Arabella took a step back and put a hand on Cinaed's arm. "He's going a little—" But before she could finish, Lucian landed roughly on the cave edge, absorbing the speed with a screech of talons digging into the granite. Then his dragon feet turned into boots, and finally, the rest of him transformed. He stood before them, looking haggard and a little wild-eyed.

"My liege—" Cinaed started.

Lucian threw him a cold look. "Leave us."

Cinaed's eyes went wide, and Arabella was right there with him. Why was Lucian acting so… *strange?*

Then his amber eyes snapped back to her. "I wish to talk to my mate alone."

Arabella struggled for something to say. On the one hand, this was exactly why she came—to talk to him—but a chill was running down her back with his gruff tone and angry demeanor. Then again, she *did* need to apologize.

Cinaed looked severely troubled. "Lucian, are you sure—"

Arabella squeezed his arm. "It's okay, Cinaed. There's something I need to talk to Lucian about… *in private.*"

Cinaed seemed thoroughly unconvinced, flicking looks back and forth between the two of them. And she could understand why—maybe Lucian's wyvern form was coming out again. But she knew he would never hurt her.

"All right, my lady," Cinaed said, his voice full of reluctance. With a nod to Lucian, he took several quick steps to the edge of the cave, leaping off and shifting just as Leksander had. Cinaed banked hard to the left and rose quickly out of sight above the mountain behind them.

Arabella turned to Lucian. "Look, I know you're upset, but before you say anything, I just want to apologize."

He arched an eyebrow. "Apologize?"

She found one of her hands pounding the other open palm silently—her nervous habit—and forced her hands to be still. "I'm sorry I brought up the sealing. I know you're still hurting over... over *Cara.*" She swallowed. His eyes took on a shine when she said his dead mate's name. She prayed she wasn't screwing up even more by bringing it up again. "I shouldn't have just rushed into that. I want to take things slow—not too slow, of course, because of your wyvern coming out—but I should let you set the pace on this. I promise I won't push anymore."

"Do you truly promise?" He edged toward her and touched her cheek with the back of his fingers

Relief gushed through her—he was *touching* her again. "I promise."

"Good." He stepped even closer. "Because I can think of something much more pleasant to do than talking." Suddenly his lips were on hers, kissing her, devouring her, pulling her against him. Her body zoomed from feeling wracked with guilt and stress and worry to *wanting* him. It was dizzying. *Of course,* she wanted him—he was gorgeous, and she loved him—but this kiss… it was so rushed and hurried and strangely aggressive.

She pulled back, and he almost didn't let her go. Her breath was heaving. She looked up into his eyes. "Do you really want to do this…" They were in his *death tomb.* What the hell? The mere idea of making love here was creeping her out.

"Don't *you* want to?" he asked with a smirk, moving in on her again. This time, he backed her up two steps until she was against the rough rock wall. It was poking into her shoulder, and she had to duck in order not to bang her head on a sharp edge that was jutting out.

But as soon as Lucian touched her cheek again, a strange lust pulsed all through her body—as if she only had one chance to have him, and that chance was *right now.* It was now or never… and *never* was not acceptable.

"Of course, I want to—" But her words were

cut off as his hand slipped to the back of her neck, and he pulled her in for another hard kiss.

Her body was saying *now now now,* but her head was clearly in *what the fuck* land.

There was something very wrong here. And if she didn't know what was going through his head when he was making love to her *before*… well, she didn't want to repeat that mistake. They needed to air this thing out before it went any further and just ruined things again.

She planted her hands on his chest and pushed him back. She had to do it three times before he finally broke the kiss.

"Lucian!" She tried to back away, but there was nowhere to go. "What are you doing?"

A sudden rush of wings beating the air heralded Cinaed's return. *"My lady!* Is everything all right?"

Arabella flushed—*shit,* Cinaed must've been eavesdropping and thought Lucian's wyvern was coming out—but before she could open her mouth and tell him everything was fine, the look on Lucian's face told her everything was *not* fine. He was glaring at Cinaed like he wanted to drill holes through his body, slowly and with lots of pain.

"I told you to be *gone.*" Then Lucian swept a hand out toward Cinaed, and the man flew backward as if punched by a giant fist. He lofted so high in the air, he had no chance of landing inside the cave. He quickly dropped below the cave lip, out of sight.

Arabella gasped. *"Oh my God!"* She started to run toward the edge of the cave, but Lucian's hand roughly grabbed her arm and hauled her back. "What the hell are you—" But when she looked back, all words fled.

The man holding her arm wasn't Lucian.

It was the fae prince.

Zephan.

Chapter Thirteen

"You want us to do *what?*"

The vampire staring him down was Acheron, sire of the Emrick coven, the closest nest of vampires Lucian could reach once he left his tomb. Acheron's face held a mystified and terrified sort of expression, but the thirty or so vampires surrounding him seemed morbidly curious as well. The warren of caves in which they lived, deep in the Canadian mountains, tasted of iron and death and sex. The lot of them turned his stomach, but that didn't matter.

He wouldn't have to endure their presence for long.

"I'm offering you my blood, Acheron," Lucian

said. "I didn't think I'd have to talk you into a little sip of dragon."

The head vampire was older than Lucian, but he appeared to have been turned when he was twenty. Vampires were forever frozen at the age of their turning, not even showing the slow signs of aging that dragons experienced. Lucian was at the end of his life at five hundred years, while Acheron was closer to a thousand and would probably live hundreds more, all while appearing like he just learned how to shave.

But looks were deceiving, especially in the immortal world.

Acheron's eyes were completely black, so he was well fed, but that didn't explain the hesitation. "To be clear," he said stiffly, "you're not offering *a little sip*, Prince of the House of Smoke. You're offering to commit suicide. Or did I misunderstand? Because the last thing I want is to misunderstand in something that will bring a horde of dragon talons down on my coven."

"You didn't misunderstand," Lucian said.

"Why exactly do you want to die?"

"That's my problem, not yours." He shifted one hand into talons, and the crowd of vampires leaned back. Acheron, to his credit, didn't move a single muscle. Lucian quickly slashed one of his wrists, then the other—his hands were fast covered in blood. The vampires leaned forward again, and he knew the scent of it must be boiling the *want* in their veins.

The Emrick coven was deep in the wilds of Canada, and supposedly, they only fed off animals. And even that was far more civilized than it sounded. They hunted the animals, drained them of their blood, and stored it for later consumption. In a way, they were no different than any other human-type species that hunted animals for food, which included a good fraction of humanity for most of history. The vampires were part of the natural ecosystem of their territory and kept a careful balance between themselves and the nature surrounding them—which didn't make them any less nauseating to Lucian, given their preference would always be for human blood. And now he was offering them the sweetest, most alluring taste— even among dragonkind, his blood was rare and powerful, considering he had fae magic running through it.

They were practically drooling for the fat red drops dripping off his wrists.

Acheron held them back by spreading his arms

wide. He glared at them one by one then turned back to Lucian. "How do we know this isn't some kind of trick?"

"Our agreement is that you have to leave humans alone. It says nothing about dragons. And here I am offering you an entire dragon's worth of blood. Just consider it your lucky day, and let's get on with it." He held up his wrists toward the waiting crowd, hoping they would make quick work of him. "Make it fast, before my blood clots and closes up."

The vampires were restless, but Acheron still held them back. He arched an eyebrow and stepped forward. Lucian towered over most species, vampires included—they retained all their human features, with the exception of that slightly more pale skin and those damn eyes that were inky pools of darkness. Their eyes would be even darker after they fed on him.

"So your blood clots quickly, does it?" Acheron asked, carefully.

"Just one of many reasons why I can't do this myself," Lucian grumbled. "It also regenerates quickly, so don't take too long about it."

Acheron stroked his chin and seemed to be still contemplating his options.

And Lucian didn't have that kind of time. He growled, causing the vamp to lean back a little. "Or I can take your recent incursion on the human population in Seattle as an excuse to burn down your coven with dragonfire. Then I'll move on to a coven that won't hesitate to take my blood. Choice is yours."

"Well…" Acheron held his hands up in surrender. "When you put it that way." He motioned to two vampires, one on either side of the semicircle that had formed around Lucian. The vampires—both female—quickly stumbled forward and knelt at Lucian's sides. He could see the hunger on their faces as their tongues traced their lips—they were staring at the red lines snaking down his hands, but Lucian could already feel the wounds healing. He would have to open them again. Vampire fangs weren't strong enough to pierce dragon skin on their own.

Acheron kept his hand up, clearly a signal to hold them back. "But as we're doing this service for you, Prince of the House of Smoke, I do not wish to cause discord in my coven. My mate, Callidora, and my purebred daughter, Giselle, will feast on you first. I believe you have a preference for women, am I right?"

Lucian curled a lip in disgust. He'd much prefer a clean death by talons, but that wasn't in the offing… he would have to take what he could get. Besides, the degradation of it was probably a suitable end for him, given what he was doing.

"I don't care who you pick, Acheron, but you're taking too damn long."

"Well, we'll be stretching it out a little bit—if you don't terribly mind dying a little more slowly and with a little more… *enjoyment*… than you apparently wish for. But since your blood regenerates, there should be enough for everyone." He threw a glance around the crowd. The nods of agreement quickly went around, and Lucian was sure that every last one of them was going to get their take before they would allow him to die.

"*Fine.* Let's get started." He slashed new gouges in his wrists and shoved them toward the faces of the women.

They waited until Acheron gave them a nod, but then they grabbed hold of his arms with surprisingly strong grips and sunk their teeth into his open wounds. Their cool lips latched onto his skin and pulled hard. The venom in their fangs quickly infused his flesh—he briefly hoped it wouldn't have the same effect on dragons as it did on humans, but he was quickly disabused of that idea. A sexual flush rushed through him, and his cock roared to life.

Fuck.

A wave of dizziness washed through him, and Lucian dropped to his knees, taking the women with him. A buzz started at his wrists and slowly climbed his arms. The women were ravaging his arms, but he felt nothing but pleasure flushing through him.

"Slowly, my loves," Acheron admonished them with a smirk. "Don't forget you need to share." The two women slowed the pull—somehow, they were intuiting exactly how fast they could draw him down while still having his blood replenish at an equal rate.

Then Acheron signaled another vampire from the crowd to step forward.

Lucian blinked several times then squinted. This new one was the same vampire he had pulled away from the human in Seattle—the one Leksander had cured. Only the man's eyes were no longer blue, shining the deep black of a vampire instead. "You…" Lucian's word was slurred—the venom had reached his neck, and his voice suffered for it.

"Yes, you know Draven, don't you?" Acheron

brought the vamp closer, then knelt on one knee in front of Lucian, peering at him. "That was quite some fae trickery your brother performed on my son."

Lucian blinked, his vision starting to haze. "But Leksander cured you." His words were even more garbled.

The man snorted a laugh. "*Cured* me! I'm a purebred, you bastard—"

Acheron held up a hand to shush him. "I'm sure the Prince of the House of Smoke thought he was doing you a favor." He drilled his liquid black eyes into Lucian. "And surely the dragons cannot hold it against us. If you magically deprive a vampire of his essence, Prince Lucian, you cannot expect to hold us in violation of our agreement for restoring him. There are so few of us now, and my son is a purebred at that. You, of all people, should be aware of how difficult it can be for immortals to procreate."

"I really don't give a fuck what you do." Lucian's words were strained and mashed together, but he was speaking the truth. None of this was his problem anymore.

Acheron smiled. "Perfect. Then we will give you exactly what you want. I dare say no dragon will have died quite so pleasantly before. And the fae magic in your blood will be a welcome addition to my coven."

Lucian frowned, thinking perhaps he should've thought that through more carefully before volunteering to give his blood away to a nest of vampires... but it was far too late for second-guessing.

Acheron waved away the women at his wrists, and two others replaced them. The fresh surge of venom from their fangs flushed through him and brought with it a mind-numbing amount of pleasure. His body was convulsing with it now. They laid him back on the floor, his arms spread wide, his cock pointing straight up. His mind was completely clouded over in the venom-induced haze.

His thoughts drifted away...

...*to Arabella.*

He would never have a chance to be with her again—so perhaps this last, hazy drug-fueled dream-time would be his final goodbye. He could easily picture her in bed, skin to skin with him, enjoying the exquisite pleasure he would visit upon her body. He would never have a chance to experience mated sex with her, but in his dream, he would have the fullness of it. But when he imagined it, the venom mixed everything together—Cara's soft skin; Arabella's scent; the feel of them both pulsing around him. He growled, or perhaps that was a roar coming out of his mouth and deafening his ears… he wasn't sure. But his frustration drove out the remnants of his dead mate and left only the woman he would never have. He could taste Arabella's strength. He could see the love in her eyes when she looked at him. Then all of it was lost in a throe of ecstasy that gripped him and convulsed him. He lost track of what was real and what was a dream, drowning and dying under the influence of endless waves of venom injecting pleasure into his bloodstream.

He was weakening—his blood supply must finally be dwindling, bringing its own kind of light-headedness.

He was drifting. He closed his eyes. Drifting and sailing off into the haze. Acheron was right. This was a much better way to die.

Then something hit him.

Once, twice… on the third time, he actually felt something strike his face. There was no pain and hardly even any sensation. But something was definitely hitting him, and the hitting was definitely occurring on his face.

Lucian struggled for many seconds but finally managed to open his eyes.

Cinaed was peering down at him with a look of utter disgust. "What the fuck do you think you're doing?"

The words felt like the final slap that knocked him out of his grogginess. Lucian was still laid out on the floor—he could feel the stone underneath him—but there were no more vampires attached to his wrists.

Fuck. He had failed at even this.

Lucian slowly dragged his gaze from his bloody arms back to Cinaed. "Why are you here?"

"I've come for you." Anger enlivened Cinaed's face. "I didn't realize you would fall so far so fast." His words were stabbing into Lucian's chest. And then he realized that as bad as he must look... Cinaed looked worse. Someone had beaten the shit out of his best friend—which was no small thing, given he was dragon. And a tough one at that.

Alarm broke through the last of Lucian's haze. He sat up. "What happened?"

Acheron spoke from just behind Cinaed. "Sorry, Prince Lucian, but we simply couldn't have your death on our hands. We contacted your House, and this is the dragon they sent. And it's a good thing—

Heart of a Dragon

it appears your presence is still required in the immortal realm." Acheron gave him a gentle smile.

Lucian wanted to throw curses at him, but the look on Cinaed's face stopped him cold.

"He's right," Cinaed said. "The fae have her, Lucian. She needs you."

Adrenaline spiked through him and forced him to his feet. "Arabella?" He nearly toppled over with the head rush and wooziness still flooding him.

Cinaed just gave him an angry glare. "She would never have left the keep if it weren't for you."

Fuck. "Cinaed." His voice was heavy. "Just tell me what I need to do."

His best friend nodded, sharply, like Lucian had finally come to his senses. "Follow me."

183

Chapter Fourteen

"WHAT HAVE YOU DONE TO CINAED?" ARABELLA'S voice shook, but with anger, not fear.

Well... *some* fear.

Zephan's nearly-clear eyes sparkled as she threw the words back in his face. He was still gripping her arm, holding her back from running to the edge of the cave, where he had flung Cinaed out.

"That dragon is unimportant."

"He's important to *me.*" She pulled out of Zephan's grasp and stumbled back, bracing against the rock wall. *She was trapped.* Her heart was thudding in her ears. Lucian was gone. Leksander flew away. Cinaed was no match against the power of this fae prince—what possible chance did she have for escape? But she knew more than the last time she was trapped, alone, with Zephan, the prince of the Winter Fae Court. This time, she knew the treaty forbade him from killing humans… and that the fae held themselves bound to this law like it had real magic behind it.

She straightened up and gave Zephan a hard stare. She was still a lawyer, and negotiating the finer points of the law was what she did for a living. At least until she found herself at the epicenter of an insane magical tug-of-war between species far more powerful than herself.

And that was key—*humans* were at the center of this. Specifically, *her.* Well, Lucian, really, but her by proxy. Which meant she held some cards in this crazy, high-stakes poker game.

She could work with that.

Zephan was coolly examining her as she stood next to the wall. "You're a beautiful woman, Arabella. You can tell yourself that you didn't enjoy my touch, but you would be lying."

She narrowed her eyes. "You were using some kind of magic to trick me."

"Exactly." A small smile played across his face, but he didn't come any closer.

She leaned back, wary. "What do you mean by that?"

"How much of what you see with your eyes can you actually believe?" He casually crossed the distance between them, coming close enough to touch her but holding back.

"Apparently, zero with you." She had to fight the urge to make a run for the front of the cave. There was literally nowhere to go. She was perched on the edge of a cliff.

"I used a simple glamour trick." He smiled, and then his cool ice-blue eyes and pale, angular face disappeared, replaced by Lucian's amber eyes and strong cheeks.

Her heart leaped, and she couldn't help reacting to seeing him, even if she knew it was a trick. Zephan-as-Lucian reached out to touch her, and she could swear it felt exactly as it did when the real Lucian ran his fingers along her cheek. She twisted her head away.

"How much of what you feel can you trust?" He leaned forward, placing a hand on the wall behind her head and peering into her eyes with a heart-stopping look, the kind Lucian gave her that make her hunger for him. The kind that made her fall in love with him. "I can hear your heart racing, little human. You know who I am, and yet a simple trick of the eyes, and your body betrays you. Trust me… I could have you at any moment. With or without the glamour."

She swallowed. "Is this how you get every woman into your bed? Trickery, magic, and lies?"

His eyes went cold, and suddenly they were ice-blue again. He had dropped the glamour, but he was still crowding her against the wall. "You humans think you're so intelligent. That you make your own choices and decide your own fate. But the truth is you're just a bundle of chemicals and hormones surging around inside that delicate, mortal body of yours." He touched her cheek again, and a surge of lust raged through her body, making her gasp. Heat pooled between her legs, horrifying her, yet making her crave his touch down there at the same time. It was terrifying, this literal magical control he had over her body. He leaned closer, as if to kiss her, but stopping just short. She almost bridged the gap herself, and only through an insane amount of willpower did she hold back. "Lucian's touch gets you hot," he whispered. "But mine will make you melt into a puddle of wanton desire. You may think it's love that's binding you to him, but it's nothing more than hormones, my dear. A chemical soup of neurotransmitters that I can manipulate with just a touch and a taste of magic."

"Leave… me… *alone.*" It took everything she had to breathe those words out between her teeth.

He pulled back, taking his touch with him, and the heat dropped out of her body like a cork had been pulled at her feet.

"I'm not even trying all that hard, Arabella," he said coolly, a smirk on his face. "If I wanted you, I'd have you right up against this wall. And you'd be begging for more."

"Say what you want." Her body was still heaving with the after effects of the lust haze he'd induced in her. *"Do* what you want to me. But none of it will change how I feel about Lucian."

His eyes flashed, and suddenly, she could see it —*that* was the core of all this.

He wanted to pull her away from Lucian.

No matter what happened, she vowed in that moment not to let him succeed.

"Are you quite sure about that?" His eyes were sparkling again as if he enjoyed the challenge as much as anything. Maybe immortal life was super-boring, and he got off on messing with people's heads. Maybe he was just an asshole. Or maybe there were deeper reasons why he wanted to disrupt the treaty between the fae and the dragons.

Arabella didn't know, she couldn't figure it out

for sure, and it didn't matter anyway. All she knew was that *no way in hell* was the only proper response for whatever Zephan was trying to accomplish here.

"I'm very sure of my love for Lucian." Arabella threw the challenge back at him. "And I'm not an idiot, Zephan. I know what you're trying to do here, and I know all about the treaty. Maybe you can mess with my hormones, but you should be careful about underestimating a human. Especially one you have trapped up against a wall. We're not as stupid as you seem to think."

He arched an eyebrow. "Do you think you're the first human I've taken to my bed?"

"No, I'm sure you got good at being an asshole through diligent practice." She gave him her best look of loathing.

A smirk blossomed on his face. "Cara said almost the same thing."

Arabella choked for a moment, her air suddenly cut off at the mention of Lucian's dead mate. Then she spat out the words surging through her head. *"You did this to Cara?"*

His smirk grew. "She was all too happy to moan and writhe in my bed. Pregnant women aren't normally my thing, but I'll admit to enjoying that one. Especially the crying afterward."

Horror left her mouth hanging open. Then she forced it shut. "You're lying."

Anger clouded his eyes for a moment, then he leaned in fast and threatening.

Arabella plastered back against the rocky wall, banging her head as she went, but that look in his eyes... it was like he wanted to shred her apart, molecule by molecule.

"A fae never lies." His hiss was visceral and sent a shiver through her. Then his anger cooled as fast as it had appeared. "Didn't your dragon lover tell you? Oh right... *dragons lie.* But the fae are incapable of it. Just one of our many sterling personal qualities. We always tell the truth, Arabella—it's just that the truth is so awful sometimes, so horrible, that people don't want to believe it. And the truth is that Cara's pregnancy failed because she doubted her love for Lucian—and the peculiarities of this magical treaty they live under made that a capital offense. Barbaric if you ask me, but I've been saying that for some time about this *infernal* treaty. But I understand her doubt—it's a wonder to me that she survived as long as she did. Lucian's broken in a way that cannot be fixed, Arabella. A way that has him finding pleasure in the most degraded of ways." He leaned back and waved his hand at the rocky wall

next to her head. It shimmered and disappeared, with a round portal to another place appearing instead. It was like a window straight into another cavern, only this one was dark and flickering with low light. *And what she saw…*

Arabella reflexively covered her mouth with her hand, holding in her gasp.

Lucian was writhing on the ground, moaning in a way that was definitely *not* pain. Two women were bent over him, their mouths latched onto his wrists. She didn't know what exactly they were doing, but there was no mistaking Lucian's king-sized erection tenting out his pants.

"Vampires," Zephan spat. "Disgusting creatures. Like having sex with a Carnal Class demon. Not that I would know… I conjure them, I don't fuck them." He wiped away the portal or vision or whatever it was. "Lucian is forever marked by the death of his mate… *a death he caused.* He'll lie about that in ways he probably doesn't even recognize as lying. I, on the other hand, am a Prince of the Winter Fae Court. By definition, you'll always have the truth from me… and more pleasure than you can stand."

"I want nothing to do with you. *Ever.*" But there was a cloud over her heart. Why was Lucian with those vampires? What was he doing? Was he running so hard from her—from the possibility of loving her and losing her—that he was resorting to *that* in order to forget her? A black, inky ooze in her chest almost made her believe it. *This is doubt,* she told herself. *This is what you have to not do.* She steeled herself against that black feeling, staring hard at the mountains outside the cave and hoping she could hold out against all of Zephan's tricks. *Lucian, where are you?* she couldn't help thinking.

"Don't you wonder why Lucian carries such guilt over the death of his mate?"

Arabella whipped her gaze back to Zephan, who was still leaning entirely too close. "It's natural for someone to blame themselves when bad things happen."

He shook his head. "That's not it. Lucian's had decades to get over this, Arabella. *Decades.* He carries the burden of guilt because it truly is his fault. He failed to keep his mate safe. Just as he's failed to keep you safe. Where is he now, exactly? Oh right, getting off with vampires. Cara died because she *doubted* her love for him… and there was a very good reason for that. He failed her. And he'll fail you, too."

Those words… somehow those words rang through Arabella's entire body like a clarion. Like an enormous bell had rung deep in her soul. She didn't have magic like dragons or fae, but she felt something inside her shift, strong and hard and with a sizzling energy that *felt* magical.

She planted her hands on Zephan's chest and pushed— not to move him, but to shove herself away. Then she jabbed a finger at him. "You stay the hell away from me!" She heaved as that soul-deep feeling blossomed and grew and filled every fiber of her being. It was a recognition of what Zephan truly was, and how she felt, deep in her soul, about Lucian. He was everything good and right and noble in the world, no matter how broken he might be right now… and maybe forever. Lucian loved hard and deep and carried the weight of the world on his shoulders, just as Cinaed said.

Zephan was a destroyer.

"*You,*" she said, jabbing at him again. "You are an evil bastard who manipulates others. I've seen dozens of men like you in my practice, every day, preying on women, twisting their minds, their hearts, and their souls. You're the worst kind of vampire—you don't just suck away the life from someone; you take what's good inside them and twist it into evil. You destroy them for your own fucked-up purposes. And then you turn it around on them and convince them that they're to blame for being manipulated by you. Well, *fuck you* and every man like you, immortal or not. You stay the hell away from me. And you stay away from Lucian."

Zephan's eyes went cold and hard during her tirade. "You don't hold the cards here, Arabella. I do."

She lifted her chin. "We'll see about that." She was trembling, but it wasn't fear. It wasn't even anger. It was pure goddamn righteous *I've-had-enough-of-your-shit.* And damn if it didn't feel good.

Just as Zephan lurched forward, his hand reaching for her, Arabella heard a screaming roar like nothing she'd ever heard in her life. She and Zephan both looked to the front of the cave where the terror-inducing sound had come from.

Three shapes were speeding like rockets through the air straight toward them.

Chapter Fifteen

LUCIAN ITCHED TO FLY FASTER, BUT CINAED NEEDED to reach Arabella first.

Still… the runes on his body writhed with the need to reach his tomb, and that propelled him ahead by inches and more inches. Leksander kept pace with him using fae-boosted power, but Cinaed was struggling to keep up, even with all his dragon-fueled strength. Lucian's need to go faster nearly strangled him as they finally came within sight of the tomb.

That damn fae has his hands on her.

Hold back, my brother. Leksander's words slammed into Lucian's head. *Stay with the plan.*

Lucian released a stream of dragontongue curses on his brother's mind but held back from racing ahead to yank Arabella from Zephan's embrace. Lucian would be there in seconds… and then he would make Zephan pay for touching her. Suddenly, Arabella pushed away from the fae prince, yelling at Zephan about something.

When the prince lunged for her, Lucian couldn't hold back any longer.

He let loose a primal, dragon scream that meant, *Hands off my mate.* The sound ripped across the air, reaching the tomb before him and succeeding in yanking Zephan's attention away from whatever harm he planned to visit upon Arabella. The three of them—Lucian, Leksander, and Cinaed—put on a burst of speed, and less than two long seconds later, they were crashing in on the tomb.

A blur of blue to his side was Cinaed taking Arabella.

She yelped as he grabbed her, but Lucian knew he would get her safely out of the tomb. Lucian's focus was all for the fae bastard his talons were crashing down upon. The prince jumped back, barely eluding Lucian's slicing grip, but Lucian's speed caught him anyway. He crashed into the fae, taking him sailing back into the dark crevices of the cave. The treaty said the fae couldn't kill anyone from the House of Smoke… but it said nothing about dragons killing fae. Never mind that it was damn near impossible—Lucian would give it a hell of a try.

Zephan hurled some magical force against him, but Lucian was already sinking his talons into the bastard's slim fae body. He was slippery, like an eel, but the magical force the fae was hurling lost its power with Lucian anchored to the fae himself, and the pain provided a powerful distraction.

Zephan roared and finally hurled Lucian off him, sending him crashing against a rocky wall. But they were well to the back of the cave, which was precisely where Lucian needed to keep him. At least for a few moments—as long as it would take Leksander to do his work. Lucian rushed at Zephan again, but the fae was ready for him this time. A flick of the wrist sent Lucian crashing back into the same wall. Zephan wiped blood from his side and glared at the bluish substance. *Holy mother of magic,* did the fae actually bleed magic? Lucian had never seen the blood of one before. No matter—Lucian hurled himself at Zephan again, this time sending a torrent of dragonfire ahead. Zephan blocked that stream, curling it back around to blast Lucian with his own dragonfire, but Lucian's momentum carried him through the burning baptism to once again crash against the fae, hurling them both against the back wall. Lucian got in a few more good slices, bloodying his talons with Zephan's thick, blue muck before the fae recovered from the stun and sent Lucian hurtling against the opposite wall again.

Zephan quickly stood. "As much fun as this is, I'm growing tired of this game." He gathered a ball of magical energy that crackled with miniature lightning bolts and hurled it at Lucian. He had nowhere to go and took the full brunt of it on his chest. Lucian could feel the scales burning, and he howled through the pain, but once it was spent, he managed to stagger to his feet.

Zephan's normally unflappable expression was thoroughly flapped. The ire on his face alone held enough power to end Lucian's life… if such a thing were allowed by the treaty.

"I am done with this stupidity." Zephan spat blue blood on the floor.

"I don't think so," said Leksander from the front of the cave. He had shifted human and stood with his legs planted wide and his arms crossed. Lucian shifted to human as well—the magical burn marks Zephan had given him were red and angry across his chest. He conjured clothes to cover them.

Heart of a Dragon

Zephan threw a glare at each of them then turned in the way fae do when they're opening one of those interdimensional doors they use to hop and skip around the world and to otherworldly fae dimensions in between.

Only he went nowhere.

Lucian grinned at his brother, but Leksander's face was inscrutable—and his eyes were trained on Zephan. For the fae's part, his expression was one of blank surprise. He staggered a step back, then darted his gaze all over the cave.

"That's right," Leksander said. "Wards. Simple ones, really. But they're *dragon wards*… and you are fucked. Because just like wards can keep you out of our keep, guess what? You're not leaving this tomb until we take them down."

Just as Lucian had never seen a fae's blue blood before, he'd never seen fear on one's face. But a flash of it was unmistakable on Zephan's. Then his expression shut down hard and was replaced by the kind of loathing that would have ended Lucian's life on the spot if he weren't protected by the treaty.

"You cannot be serious," Zephan said, straightening and wiping his blood off his hands. "What do you think you can possibly accomplish——"

"I have one simple demand," Lucian cut him off.

Zephan whipped his gaze to Lucian, and Lucian could hear the breath wheezing in and out of Zephan's lungs, even with the stone-cold expression on his face.

"You do *not* make demands of me." There was a quaver of pure hatred. Or maybe fear. Lucian didn't care, as long as it motivated him.

"We do today," Leksander said calmly. He strolled with more casualness than Lucian could muster, his blood still boiling with the need to kill the fae that had threatened his mate, not to mention the pain still rippling across half his body from the fae's burning magical fire.

Leksander stopped in front of a decidedly shaken-looking Zephan. "You will never attempt to kidnap or harm Arabella in any way. Promise it, and we'll take down the wards and set you free."

"I don't make promises to dragons," Zephan sneered, but the wideness of his eyes and the scent of fear upon him betrayed him. His gaze darted to the outside of the cave. Cinaed clung to the edge of the cliff in dragon form, Arabella safely on his back, both of them staring, silently watching. The wards shimmered, providing a barrier between them—keeping Arabella safe and Zephan trapped. By the time Zephan's gaze came back inside the cave, Lucian could scent the defeat on him.

"Make the promise, Zephan," he growled. He knew well that the fae's promise held power—a magical bond that would literally prevent him from taking actions like today ever again.

Zephan rumbled his own growl of frustration and glared at Lucian.

"She is my mate," Lucian roared, knowing full well that the wards would keep in creatures with magic in their blood, but not the words he was sending forth. Arabella would hear them plain enough. "You will not touch her. You will not harm her. Swear it now, Zephan, or see how long you can last in a cave with two dragons descended from fae and protected by treaty. Either you will die or we will… and only one of those will break a ten-thousand-year peace."

"And it's not *your death,"* Leksander added. "Which do you think the Winter Court will abandon first—you or ten thousand years of peace with the Summer Court?"

Zephan glared with such fury that magic crackled along his skin in skittering blue wisps. For a long moment, Lucian thought he would rather fight than concede.

But then the fae prince opened his mouth and said, "By my true name, I will not touch or harm Arabella Sharp."

Relief weakened Lucian—he was already low on blood from his ill-fated time with the vampires, and this reprieve threatened to send him to his knees.

"Good enough?" Leksander asked, giving Lucian a sideways look.

Lucian was sure his brother wanted to press for more, but it *was* enough... all he needed was for Arabella to be safe. And they were skating close to war as it was—all of this was a calculated gamble.

"Take down the wards." Lucian restrained himself from bracing against the nearby wall. He willed himself to stay upright at least until the fae left.

Leksander's runes scurried across his arms as he summoned their magic to disassemble the wards he had hastily placed when they arrived. In just a moment, they were down.

Zephan sneered at Lucian. "Your mate was delicious for the short time I had her." Then he turned and disappeared, slipping into the interdimensional door the bastards used to travel.

Lucian roared and stumbled forward to swipe at him, but he was already gone. He wanted to believe the fae bastard's words weren't true… but he knew they never lied. The exact meaning and extent of those words might be unclear, but this much he knew—Zephan's lips had been on Arabella. *He had tasted her.* And it carved a sickness deep in Lucian's soul.

Then he saw the worried look on Arabella's face —Cinaed had brought her into the cave as soon as the wards were down—and all Lucian could think of was having her in his arms… and whether Zephan had already poisoned that too much. Or Lucian himself had. Could she even love him at all with what had happened… much less with a love that was True?

"Arabella." A wave of dizziness caught him, and he barely grabbed hold of a rocky lip of the wall to keep himself upright.

Cinaed had been holding her back, but now she rushed forward to Lucian's side. "Oh my God, are you all right?" Her soft hands were on him, touching the arm that was half charred from

ALISA WOODS

Zephan's attack. He couldn't help wincing, and she noticed. "Oh God, I'm hurting you!"

Lucian smiled. "No. Not even close." He reached out and pulled her into his arms. She curled into him, and the feel of that was insanely glorious—like his own piece of heaven on earth. *She was safe. She was his.* The fact that she wasn't shying away from him was like a breath of new life. And she was even wearing some kind of white and flowing gown… *a sealing garment.* It was like a sign from the universe blessing this horrible thing he knew he had to do. He pulled back enough to take her soft cheeks in his hands. He realized too late that his hands were still covered with Zephan's blood, not to mention his own. He ignored that and peered into her eyes. "Tell me he didn't hurt you."

"He didn't hurt me," she said solemnly. "I think I might have hurt his feelings, though."

A laugh welled deep inside Lucian. Keeping it inside meant a supreme force of will. Instead, he just smiled. "You're in my arms, now. That's all that matters."

But she frowned at that, and it tore into his heart. Had he already lost her?

He would know soon enough.

Because he was done running… and fae-promise or no, he didn't trust Zephan not to try again, in some duplicitous fae manner, to take Arabella into his realm and never return. Maybe Zephan was trying to break the treaty. Maybe he was simply fucking with Lucian because he had nothing better to do with his eternal fae lifetime. Maybe he had truly gotten a taste of Arabella and knew what an extraordinary woman she was.

It could be any of those things, and ultimately, it didn't matter.

Mating with Lucian would almost certainly kill her… but she wasn't safe without him by her side, either.

And he was responsible for putting her in that position. Once Lucian sealed her, Zephan truly couldn't touch her again. And she would be nearly impossible to kill by any other hand… except his own.

As Cara had been.

"Let me take you home," he said softly to her.

Her smile in response nearly broke his heart.

Chapter Sixteen

"This is crazy," Rachel said. "No, this is fucking *you-need-to-be-on-meds* insane."

"Just zip me up." Arabella stood before a mirror in the guest apartment of the keep, getting dressed in a long, flowing white gown. The simple one she had worn before had absolutely nothing on this piece of magic Lucian had conjured for her. She had to shower off the grime and the sweat and every trace of the horrible touch of Zephan on her skin before she could put it on… but now that Rachel was zipping her into it, she was open-mouthed amazed at it.

The top smoothly clung to her bare skin—it was impossible to wear anything underneath—fitting snugly all through her chest and down her arms and dripping long, trailing wisps of filmy white fabric from her wrists to the floor. More of those same wispy tendrils billowed from the waist and formed a skirt of a thousand, glittering pieces. Each seemed made from glass and stardust, glinting white only because it caught the light and sparkled. Her feet were bare, and her hair was freshly washed and barely dry, just falling plain across her nearly-naked shoulders.

Lucian had given her strict instructions on how to bathe and dress to prepare.

Rachel was grumbling behind her, but she'd finally hooked the last tiny crystal latch that kept the floating, luminous dress somehow clinging to her body.

Her best friend peered over her shoulder and scowled into the mirror. "You're a fucking virgin sacrifice in this thing."

Arabella snorted ungraciously. "I'm *so* far from being a virgin."

"You know what I'm saying."

Arabella turned to her. "No, I really don't. Rachel, it's going to be fine."

"You don't *know* that." Then Rachel bit her lip,

and that worry infected Arabella's heart. Because she *didn't* know it. She could only hope. And love Lucian. And have an iron-willed determination to do both as thoroughly as it was possible to do.

"Well, I know one thing," Cinaed said from the doorway to her bedroom. He hadn't been there a moment before. "If Lucian weren't already smitten, he'd take one look at *that* and be done for." A smile danced in Cinaed's eyes.

Rachel trained her scowl on the blue dragon that had brought Lucian back to her. *"You* are the last person to get a vote on this!"

"Aye," he agreed, not rising to her bait. "There's only one vote that counts in this." He gave Arabella a soft look. "Are you ready, my lady?"

"No! She's not ready." Rachel bustled toward him, fluttering her hands at him. "Now get out!"

Cinaed didn't budge from the doorway.

"Rachel." Arabella had to say something before she left for Lucian's lair.

"No!" Rachel whirled, turning her back on Cinaed at the door. "I forbid it! You can't do this. It's insane. You're under… under…" She flailed her hands around, then flicked them accusingly toward Cinaed. "Lucian's put you under some kind of

208

dragon pheromone that's messing with your head and making you go all weak in the knees. Just because he's hot doesn't mean you have to do this, Ari!" Her best friend's eyes were beginning to glass with tears that Arabella was afraid she might actually shed. And that would just make this harder.

Cinaed laid a gentle hand on Rachel's shoulder. "She's in love—"

Mistake. Rachel turned on him and pounded a fist into his shoulder. "I don't give a fuck! And this is all *your* fault!"

"*My* fault?" His eyes went wide.

Arabella sighed. Rachel was finally getting a rise out of him. Probably not the kind she wanted, or at this point *needed,* but that was exactly what Arabella had to clear the air about. *Now…* before it was too late.

"Yes, *your* fault!" Rachel was still pounding on Cinaed's chest. "You went off and made this whole thing happen, and now she's convinced that she has to do this thing to save the world, and it's all a load of crap! You damn, sexy dragons and all your magic can just go to hell!"

"Is that right?" His eyes were lighting up in that way that said he was either going to kiss her or stalk off really pissed. And neither one was good at the moment.

"Hello?" Arabella called, striding toward them. "Remember me? The virgin sacrifice? Let's stay focused, people."

Cinaed grimaced, but Rachel... her friend just sobbed and threw her arms around Arabella. Which only brought tears to her eyes, and that was *not* how she wanted this to go. She extricated herself from Rachel's clinging grasp.

"I'm going to become Lucian's mate—"

"*No!*"

"And I might die doing it."

Rachel twisted up her lips like she wanted to say something but couldn't.

Arabella put her hands on Rachel's shoulders. "You know I love you. You're the only family I've ever had, Rach, so I need two things from you."

Rachel blinked fast, but she could see her friend rising to the occasion, and Arabella had never been so proud of her. Or loved her so much.

"Two things," Rachel repeated like she was ready for her orders.

"First, I'll need you here when it's all over." Arabella smiled a little. "I'm going to be a mama to a dragonling, and that's some crazy shit right there.

I'm going to need help. I *need* you, Rach. Act together, shit wired. Got it?"

She nodded rapidly, and fresh tears fell. "I'll be right here."

"And second…" She flicked a look to Cinaed, who was paying rapt attention. "If I don't come back, I want you to know that it's okay with me."

Cinaed, safely behind Rachel's back, had a look of relief on his face.

But Rachel's was still scrunched up with worry and tears. *"What's* okay?"

Arabella peered into her friend's eyes. "For you and Cinaed to, you know, get wild in the sheets."

Her eyes went wide. "What? I'm not…" She twisted back to look at Cinaed, who was working hard to rein in his smirk. "I am *not*—repeat *not*—banging this asshole who talked my best friend into her death." She glared at him. "Don't even fucking think about it."

He held up his hands and back away. "Wouldn't dream of it."

"You better *not* be dreaming of it." She was ramping up again. But Arabella guessed Cinaed had been true to his word, and the two of them *hadn't* yet gotten together.

Very much *yet* with that, she suspected, especially now that she'd given him the go-ahead.

But Cinaed just shook his head and kept backing down the hall. When he was halfway to the front door, he stopped. "It's time, my lady," he said to Arabella. "If you're ready."

"I am."

Rachel whipped back to face her, and Arabella hugged her hard. *"Goddamn you,"* Rachel whispered. "I hate you so much."

Arabella smiled. "I know." She had to pry herself away, but she managed it.

Then Rachel fled into the bedroom and slammed the door in Arabella's face.

It would have hurt, but she knew Rachel too well. It was how she needed this—a clean break, just in case Arabella didn't come back.

She trudged after Cinaed to the front door.

"She doesn't mean it, my lady," he said, a deep scowl on his face for the slammed door.

She squinted at Cinaed. "You had better figure out fast that Rachel means every word she says."

He looked startled. "Then perhaps it's just the way of saying it she doesn't mean."

"Oh no, she means that, too."

He frowned and looked seriously confused, but

she didn't have any more time to worry about the two of them. At least now she knew Cinaed would watch out for Rachel… in case Arabella really *didn't* come back.

But she didn't believe that would happen. *Couldn't* believe it.

Leonidas was waiting just outside the door.

"Oh," was all Arabella said, words fleeing. *Unexpected* was an understatement.

He was dressed in a custom-tailored suit that looked ancient and very royal—like something out of the middle ages. He was drop-dead gorgeous in it, and it just served to embarrassingly remind her of their encounter before in his lair.

He offered her his arm. "My lady." To Cinaed, he said, "I'll be taking the princess from here."

Cinaed ducked his head in deference and slipped back inside Arabella's apartment.

Arabella took his arm and walked down the hallway with him, not quite successful in banishing the frown from her face. "Princess?"

"Well, not quite yet. But soon," Leonidas said smoothly, no hint of the sexy tone he had used with her before. "I know you know the way to Lucian's lair… I just wanted to steal a chance to apologize."

"Apologize?" She lifted her eyebrows but waited for him to go on.

"For things I may or may not have done previously." He smirked a little, but then it was gone. "I want you to know that you and Lucian have my every blessing. I want nothing but True Love between you. And for what it's worth, I think you already have it. I've never seen a dragon more in love with a woman than my brother is with you."

She fought to hold back her smile. "I thought you didn't know what love was."

His face was deadly serious as they pulled up to Lucian's door. "I don't. But if I ever wanted to imagine what it might look like, I need only look at your face, and his, to know." Then he reached forward, gently held her still-damp head in both hands, and kissed her softly on the forehead. "Love him well, Arabella," he whispered.

She was surprised to feel tears dampen her lashes. "I will. I promise." Her words were equally hushed.

He smiled and turned away, leaving her to knock on the door herself.

She pulled in a breath. One final chance to leave. To say *no*, she wasn't going to risk her life just to love a man. And possibly save the world. But this wasn't just any man. This was a golden dragon. And a prince of the House of Smoke.

This was Lucian—the man who saved her life, won her heart, and made her fight like hell to win his.

And now she finally had it.

She knocked on the door… and waited.

Chapter Seventeen

THE RITUAL SHOWER CLEANSED LUCIAN'S BODY BUT not his mind.

He stepped from the steaming bathroom into the cooler bedroom and conjured clothes. His burns had healed in the travel back to the keep. His reflection in the wall screen arrested him. It was dark—a reflection in black glass—and his black wedding jacket brocaded with golden thread haunted him. There was no time for formalities. Who knew how long he had before turning wyvern for good? If Arabella survived the sealing, they could indulge in whatever ceremonies they wished after the fact, during the two-month pregnancy that would follow. There would be plenty of time to present her to the House, as well as the queen and king—although

Leksander said she had already met them. Still, he would give her every formality, every party, every beautiful thing on earth…

If she lived.

He squeezed his eyes shut and pressed his fist to his forehead. He had to banish these thoughts from his head to have any chance of success. The sealing had to be forged in *love* not *fear*… but a black sort of terror was all that filled his heart. He couldn't banish it, no matter what he tried. He hesitated a long time, lingering in his room, but eventually the quiet of his lair gave away a distant, soft knock at the door.

She was here.

He strode quickly from the bedroom, down the stairs, and through the great room, hurrying as if leaving her alone for even a moment at the door of his lair might result in her being kidnapped or whisked away by some dark malevolence that seemed to hunger after him in this cursed life.

But when he opened the door… she was still there.

"Holy mother of magic." The words had escaped his lips before his thoughts had properly registered in his brain. He had conjured the dress for her, of course, but with her in it… the delicious curves of

her body barely held back, only tantalizingly covered, and that fresh-scrubbed smell of hers… "You are the most beautiful creature I've ever seen." And he meant it.

She smiled, timid and perfect. "The dress is amazing."

He held out a hand. She took it. He pulled her inside his lair. *Inside his lair…* exactly where she belonged and where she should always call home from this moment forward.

"The dress is spectacular." His voice was already husky with the need for her. "But the woman in it is divine."

She gasped a little, but that parting of her lips was too much temptation. He crashed his lips down on hers, pressing her and her infinitely soft dress against the wall next to his door, which had barely fallen closed. His hands roamed her body, skimming the softness of the dress but seeking out the even more soft feel of her bare skin. She moaned into his mouth, and her hands clutched at the velvet of his jacket, reminding him both that he had far too many clothes on, and that he couldn't rush this. There were things that needed saying before they started, and devouring her two steps inside the door simply wasn't acceptable.

He forced himself to break the kiss and pull back.

"Arabella, there are some things..." His breath was already ragged, and the emotion threatened to reach up and choke him. "Things that need to be said..."

"Things like *I love you?* Because I do. *Fiercely,* Lucian Smoke. And I want this—I want *you*—more than I have words for."

Her words made his heart soar and ache at the same time. He touched her beautiful hair, letting his fingers say what he wanted to express as they trailed softly through. He choked back the lump in his throat. "You'll get your wish, my sweet Arabella. But you may wish you hadn't."

She *smiled* at him. So insanely brave this woman was. "There are no *regrets* in this," she said. "Either I try to love you and succeed... or I try and fail. And if I fail, well, I won't have long to regret it."

His chest squeezed, hard. "I was willing to let the world burn to save you, Arabella. I would have done it..."

She laid a finger across his lips, stilling them. "Shh. I know you love me, Lucian Smoke." Her voice was soft. She had inched up on him, leaning close and peering up into his eyes. "I know you would have given everything, even things you didn't have any right to give, to save me. I figured that out, even before Cinaed explained it all to me. But that's not the man I fell in love with. The man I love is the one who is so brave, so selflessly brave, that he would risk losing the woman he loves to save the world."

"If I lose you, my love… I am done." He could hardly speak.

Her eyes shone with unshed tears. "I know." She smiled that angelic smile again. "That's why I have to live. For both of us."

He pulled her into his arms, ducking to nuzzle against the fresh-washed scent of her hair. "If there's some kind of heaven as the angels say, then I will see you there. Because I won't last long in this world if you're not in it."

She pulled back to grip his cheeks in her soft hands. "That's *not* going to happen. Because I love you too damn much. And if there's something I've learned about this crazy, magical world of yours, it's that *love matters*. Love is everything."

"*You* are my everything." Then he reached down to scoop her into his arms. If he didn't get her to the bedroom soon, they would begin in the entranceway… and that wasn't good enough for this. Or for her. "Do you remember?" he asked as he started to carry her up the stairs. "Or do I need to explain the steps?"

She grinned. "First, you make mad love to me. Then the sealing. Then I have the best sex of my life—and you should know, Lucian Smoke, I'm going to hold you to that part. So no holding back."

He crossed the threshold to his bedroom. "No holding back." And with that, his heart soared, finally unshackled from all the worry and pain and heartbreak. He was *all in* with Arabella. They would make this love of theirs happen—*together*—or they would both die trying. She had pledged her heart already in a wholehearted way that he had shied from, held back from, avoided, rationalized, and damn near destroyed the world in an attempt to stop.

And she had simply given her heart to him.

He was unabashedly clear about how undeserving he was of her and her love—and yet, it was the very thing that would keep the world going, both his and everyone else's. And he had finally figured out, not a moment too soon, that he had to save the world in order to have any chance of saving *her*.

And now, in this moment, there was nothing but

her love and his, together, begging for the sacred consummation that raised it to something far beyond sex, far beyond a bodily satisfaction, into a loud pronouncement to the world—magical and otherwise—that this feeling they held in their hearts was True. The kind of Truth that held a world-saving power all its own.

With a flick of his hand, Lucian magicked away his formal attire, and a mere wish made Arabella's gossamer gown disappear. Her quick intake of breath became even sharper as he laid her back on the bed, sliding his body against hers, skin against skin. His hard-on was already raging, and her perfume—the arousal, the scrubbed skin, the simple scent of *her*—was all one heady mix that had him ready to take her fast and hard. But that wasn't what she needed, or really, even what he wanted.

He eased up to gently kiss her on the lips, which were already parted and panting. Then he gently nipped at them, then her cheeks, and her chin. Between tastes, he said, "I want to hear you, Arabella. Every moan. Every scream. I know every inch of your body, and I'm going to make every part of you mine tonight."

"Oh, yes. *Yes.*" Her words were a prayer.

He slipped a hand down to her sex, and she was

already wet for him. His resolve to go slow was quickly dissolving. When he slipped a finger inside her, she arched up, thrusting her breasts tantalizingly close to his mouth. He dipped down and lavished attention on her already stiff nipples. She clung to him, running those soft hands over his arms and clawing at his back as he thrust a second finger in and picked up the pace. He was still nibbling on her breast, working her sex, and wondering how long he could last like this when she started begging him to take her.

"No, no, my love," he whispered, tasting his way down her belly to the slick heat between her legs. "You first."

"Oh, God," she moaned, but all argument ceased when his tongue reached her nub and circled as fast as he was thrusting inside her. He was building a rhythm that had her bucking underneath him, screaming out his name, and making his cock ache. The sweetness that was her filled his every sense—he tasted her with his fae abilities as well as with his tongue, burying his face and his mind in her body and soul. He'd made her come so many times before in this very bed—he knew every twitch and moan, the soft whimper right before the shiver and quiver of female flesh that said she was near. He palmed her gorgeous breast, kneading it while he clamped down with his mouth and plunged deep with his hand—he was playing a symphony of pleasure on her body, and the sweet song of ecstasy ramped up and up, finally reaching a peak that had her screaming and writhing and convulsing underneath him. *Holy magic,* he would never get enough of that sound, that feel of her giving herself over completely to him, letting him take her to her peak and shove her right over it.

"Oh, God," she panted. "That was just... *holy fuck,* Lucian." Her words were a little slurred with pleasure.

He just grinned. "I'm only getting started, my love."

She swallowed and nodded, but she was limp with the pleasure he'd given her. Limp and ripe and ready for his aching cock to plunge deep. Once he took her this way, the sealing would be next, so no matter what, he needed to take her higher than she'd ever gone before. That meant no rest, no pause, straight on to possessing her body and making her his.

He eased up her body, hooking his arms under her legs as he went and spreading her wide. Now her beautiful body was splayed beneath him, wide open and ready, and by pulling her knees practically up to her chest, he could plunge in deep and hard. His cock was already nudging her entrance, just from the position he was in, but he pulled back slightly so he could piston into her hard and fast and by surprise.

Her eyes flipped wide open. "Oh fuck!"

He'd sunk to the hilt in her, buried so deep it made him groan. "You are *mine.*" He pulled out and slammed in again. She gasped. "Say it," he groaned.

"Yes."

He pulled out and thrust in again.

"I'm yours!" Her hands were in his hair now, clawing as she urged him even deeper.

She was so tight, and he was in so deep, that he was thoroughly losing his mind with this. She was still human, still not sealed, so he couldn't unleash the full power of what he wanted to do with her, but he sure as hell could take her deeper and harder than he ever had before. He started pumping faster and faster, the tension coiling low and deep in his belly, building hard and fast to a climax that would have him seeing stars.

As he pounded into her, her cries went incoherent and screeched higher and higher. He tried holding back, drawing it out for her, but he was crazy with her scent and her heat and her tightness.

"Come for me, my love," he panted, barely able to hold himself back.

He pounded harder, and suddenly she was coming undone around him, screaming and bucking and thrashing. He held and kept thrusting until his own climax rushed at him and whited out the world with a blinding rush of pleasure. He emptied and emptied himself into her, knowing that every drop would help pave the way for immortalizing her body. Inuring it to the sealing fire that would come. His seed would comfort and heal her, the pain of the sealing buffeted by the pleasure she had pulsing through her now. As soon as every last drop was wrenched from him, he released her legs, pulled out, and flipped her over to her belly.

Her limbs were loose with pleasure, and she just lay there, innocent and beautiful, her skin a starry sky of freckles under porcelain. He hesitated, just a moment, then he had to start *now* or he never would.

He climbed on her, sitting on her legs to keep them still and placing his palm flat on the middle of her back, between her shoulder blades. He pressed down to hold her pinned to the bed.

Then he bent forward to whisper to her. "I'm sorry, my love. This will hurt."

And then he summoned the runes to slide across his skin, up his neck, to his face, preparing for the mating dragonfire.

Chapter Eighteen

ARABELLA KNEW IT WAS COMING, BUT THE FIRST lance of fire still made her scream.

Lucian held her down, pinning her to the bed, her face buried in the rumpled comforter they hadn't bothered to take off, and it was a good thing… she couldn't help flinching and flailing against the pain that was splitting down her back. After the first shock of it, the burning settled into a steady fire that was searing a slow, twisting line into her. She tried to bite back the screaming because while it definitely fucking hurt, it wasn't unbearable. He wasn't gouging bloody chunks out of her back or anything. She'd never had a tattoo, but she imagined it was like this—only with dragonfire not tattoo needles drilling into her skin and injecting his magic there.

Lucian's magic.

He was infusing her body with it, and just that reminder of what was actually happening to her settled her down so that she could stop the screaming and just keep it to a steady moan. She couldn't see a damn thing—her hair was tossed over her face and sucked into her mouth as it lay open, panting and moaning with the pain—but she felt every inch of him touching her. The hand that held her hard against the mattress. His legs on either side of hers, encasing her in the powerful masculine muscles he possessed *everywhere.* And that dragonfire kiss, the one slowly working its way down her back, literally tattooing his love and his magic into her.

He kept going and going, tracing a curved line, and just when it had gone on long enough that her moans were starting to get away from her again, starting to ramp up to screams… *it ended.*

"Oh, my love, my love," Lucian was whispering across her skin now. His hand had moved to her hair, but he was still holding her motionless on the bed. Only now he was kissing her… *no, he was licking her.* The velvet feel of his tongue was painting hot, wet stripes of pleasure across her back, bringing a blessed relief to the burning serpentine stripe he had painted with his dragonfire. *He was using his dragon kisses to heal her.*

Her breath was still heaving, but this time in relief. He quickly worked his way from top to bottom, and then went back for another pass. By the third one, the pain was a memory, and the feel of him kissing and licking her skin was gushing wetness between her legs.

He finally came up to her ear, brushing the hair away from her face. "Speak to me, my love. Tell me the pain is gone."

"It's gone," she said, her smile fighting the bed since her face was still half-mashed against it.

"Tell me the truth." There was an agony in his voice that she could hardly stand. "I can continue with my tongue, but if dragon tears are what you need, I have plenty of those."

She frowned and twisted to see him. Sure enough, tear tracks were racing down his face. She tried to reach for him, but he still had her pinned to the bed. So she used her words instead. "Lucian, the pain is gone. Whatever you did, it worked."

Relief was visible on his face. "Then look, my love. And see your seal." He eased to the side of her body but kept his leg draped across her bottom, keeping her flat on her stomach. He brushed more hair from her face and tipped her chin for her to look up to the ceiling. In the mirror above his bed, she could see his hot naked form sprawled next to her… and on her back was the most gorgeous dragon tattoo she'd ever seen in her life. It was serpentine, drawing a long, curling S along her back that started with a dragon head on her shoulder blade and ended with a flicking, pointed tail on her behind. And it was definitely *flicking*… the entire magical tattoo writhed along her back! Almost like it was alive, but it wasn't something separate from her… she could *feel* it.

Arabella blinked, amazed. The soft whisper of her sealing dragon didn't just pulse along her skin. She could feel it seeping into her body, racing through her veins. Her entire body was heating up, like a fever was sweeping across her, raising every hair on her body.

"Lucian," she said, breathless and a little afraid. "What's happening?"

He snuggled in next to her, pulling her body up from lying flat on the bed so that she was chest-to-chest with him now, side by side. "It's my dragon-fire," he said, amber eyes blazing into hers. "It's flushing through your body." He ran a hand along her dragon, tracing it down her back with his gentle touch. "I infused you with my magic, but it will take a few minutes to spread completely throughout." His face was intent on hers, his hand ghosting up to touch her face. He leaned in to kiss her gently on the lips, once, then twice. "It will feel like a fever consuming you for a few minutes."

And it did. The heat just kept growing. She wasn't sweating—but her skin was radiating heat like a thousand degree oven. "How hot will it get?" she asked, gasping a little because the heat was suffocating.

Fresh tears glistened in Lucian's eyes. "Very hot." Then he pressed his lips together, but he still held her gaze, petting her hair. "I'm here, my love. I'm right here."

Oh, God, this is it, she thought. This was where she would either survive the sealing… or burn up with it. And her skin kept heating, every part of her burning like a white hot sun had suddenly been born deep in her soul. *It was burning her from the inside out.* Only the heat didn't hurt—it was more like she'd stepped into the Mojave desert with an endless dry-heat expanse overwhelming her with its deadly blaze of sun.

Every part of her was on fire now, straight down

to her fingertips. She pressed them to Lucian's cheek, marveling at how he suddenly felt *cool*… when his touch had always been sexy hot.

"You better look out," she said, her breath wheezing from the fire down deep in her lungs. "You're not going to be the only hot dragon in this bed anymore."

He smiled and almost laughed, but it looked more like crying.

"Hey, it's okay," she said, tracing her fingers over his lips.

He just shook his head.

She slid one of those red-hot fingertips up to the corner of his eye—the coolness of his tears was like a balm of relief. "Dragon tears," she whispered, then she leaned forward and pressed her lips to his eyelids, kissing them as he closed them. She kissed the tears as they flowed down his cheeks, each touch bringing more coolness to her lips. Then the cool feeling spread to her face and neck and further down. When she'd dried all his tears, she touched her lips to his. "Kiss me," she whispered against them.

He did, so gently that she could hardly feel their whisper touch. "Harder," she said.

He pulled back and blinked. Once then twice.

Then he pulled her closer and kissed her like he meant it. The touch of his mouth cooled the heat in hers. His tongue was a darting relief inside her, and everywhere he touched brought more balm to her raging fire.

"More," she gasped. "Here," she said, pulling away from his kiss and baring her neck.

He moaned and feasted on her neck, taking the heated flesh in his teeth, running his tongue along it and cooling it with his wet kisses.

"Oh, God, *yes,*" she cried. "Everywhere, Lucian. Touch me everywhere."

His guttural moan and fervent kissing—down her chest, across her belly, over her arms and out to her fingertips—was exciting her like nothing ever had. He was covering her in wet kisses, and while it was quenching the too-hot fire of the sealing, it was also sparking an urgent need to have him ravish her, claim her, finish the sealing by planting his seed deep inside her.

When he'd reached the soles of her feet and kissed his way back up over her bottom and her back, Lucian pulled her around to face him again. There was such radiant joy on his face, it made her want to weep.

"Oh, my love," he cried. *"You are mine."*

And she didn't have to ask what he meant—*she knew.* She had survived the sealing. The danger was past, and there was nothing left but the urgent need to complete it—to join their bodies together and create a baby from the pureness of their love.

She grabbed hold of his rock-hard cock looming between them, giving it a quick stroke. "Take me." Her words were breathless with need. She kept pumping him, hard. *"Claim me,* Lucian."

His groan was half roar. He ripped her hand from his cock and roughly turned her over on the bed. He hauled her up on her knees, pressing his hand to her dragon seal and pushing her face into the bed. It was rough and demanding and sexy as hell—her body was thrilling to every touch. She could feel a new strength pulsing through her, a toughness in her body that was unlike anything she'd ever felt before. She craved the full strength of his hands gripping her hips, and when he plunged his cock into her, taking her from behind so hard she had to clutch the mattress to not be hurtled forward, she had only one thought: *harder.*

"Yes, my love," he cried.

She must have said that out loud.

She smiled, but it only lasted a second as Lucian gripped her hair in one hand and her hip in the other and began slamming into her like he never had before. He was *unleashed,* wild and roaring and driving his enormous cock into her, filling her completely. Every thrust sent an insane spike of pleasure through her, driving her to climax again and again until she was awash in an endless series of waves pulsing through her. The joyful abandon of his lovemaking thrilled her heart as much as her body. *She had done it!* She'd survived. And in surviving, she had healed this broken man so that he could love—he could love *her*—again.

Another guttural cry ripped out of him, and he plunged deep inside her one more time, holding still. His hot seed gushed, and she could feel it in a way she never had before—his magic was bonding with hers. His seed was quelling that final fire, the one still raging deep inside her, and together they were forming a new fire. A new life.

A baby dragon made of pure love and magic and ecstasy.

Lucian panted above her, still buried deep and holding her, but spent. Her orgasms had been so endless, her entire body was one giant buzzing pleasure zone… and that was before the baby. Now there was a quickening inside her, a humming that brought a new sense of aliveness to every fiber of her being. Even when Lucian left her body, a piece of him remained behind. And forever would.

He slumped to the bed beside her. *"Holy fuck,"* he breathed.

"I completely agree." Her smile felt like it could never be big enough to hold all her happiness. She snuggled into him as he lay prone on the bed staring up at the mirror above them.

Then he turned to her with a look of awe. He held her cheek for a moment and stared into her eyes before kissing her so tenderly she thought her heart would melt from the love of it.

When he pulled back, he searched her eyes. "Do you feel it?"

"The baby? Yes. He's beautiful. I can feel it already."

Lucian's mouth worked, but no words came out. His eyes glistened again.

She curled into him and touched his cheek with her fingertips—they were now the same temperature, hot on hot, or cool on cool, she couldn't tell which. But it didn't matter where his body ended, and hers began. They were *one* now.

"Hey, no more tears," she whispered with a smile. "I don't need any more healing."

He pulled her in for a fast and fervent kiss.

Impossibly, his cock was already growing hard between them.

She pulled her leg over his hip, grinding the wet heat of her core against the silky steel of his shaft. "However, I can definitely use some more of that."

He suitably groaned and moved with her. He gave her a half-lidded look filled with lust and love and an illegal amount of hotness. "You know what pregnancy does to a woman who is mated to a dragon?"

"I'm pretty sure it makes her crave hard and hot sex."

He grinned. "It makes her almost as insatiable as her mate."

"You mean I can finally keep up with you?" She bit her lip, but she could already feel it was true. "God, we're never leaving this bed, are we?"

"Not if I can help it."

Before she could say another word, he rolled her on her back and took her with one swift stroke, burying himself deep inside her. He had her hands pinned above her head and was pounding into her before she could even take another breath. In an instant, she was moaning and writhing under him, begging for another of what promised to be an endless number of orgasms.

When she was merely human, he was able to satisfy her like no man ever had.

Now that she was sealed with his dragonfire, it was as if her body were *made* for the kind of love-making only he could dish out. She let herself get lost in the first crashing orgasm, floating away on the pleasure he was giving her. Even in the bliss, she knew this wasn't the end of the danger—it was only the beginning. She would have to survive the pregnancy, give birth to a dragonling, and never once stumble… never once doubt.

She couldn't merely love this man—she had to make sure that, in all that time, her love was *True*. And for a woman who had never known the truth of Love before, that scared her… and not just a little.

But at this moment, joined with Lucian, floating on the bliss of being with him, she couldn't imagine anything that could take the happy dream of True Love from her. And if anything tried…

…she would fight it to the death.

She would protect her love and her baby with every last breath she had.

Lucian and Arabella's story continues in…

FIRE OF A DRAGON

(Fallen Immortals 3)

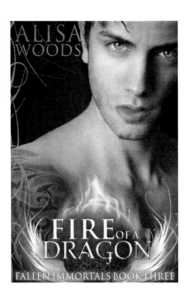

Grab Fire of a Dragon today!

Subscribe to Alisa's newsletter

for new releases and giveaways

http://smarturl.it/AWsubscribeBARDS

About the Author

Alisa Woods lives in the Midwest with her husband and family, but her heart will always belong to the beaches and mountains where she grew up. She writes sexy paranormal romances about complicated men and the strong women who love them. Her books explore the struggles we all have, where we resist—and succumb to—our most tempting vices as well as our greatest desires. No matter the challenge, Alisa firmly believes that hearts can mend and love will triumph over all.

www.AlisaWoodsAuthor.com

Manufactured by Amazon.ca
Acheson, AB